Hamilto

S0-BZA-309

Too Many Men

Lorna Schultz Nicholson

James Lorimer & Company Ltd., Publishers
Toronto

© 2006 Lorna Schultz Nicholson

All rights reserved. No part of this book may be reproduced or transmitted in any form or by any means, electronic or mechanical, including photocopying, or by any information storage or retrieval system, without permission in writing from the publisher.

James Lorimer & Company Ltd. acknowledges the support of the Ontario Arts Council. We acknowledge the support of the Government of Canada through the Book Publishing Industry Development Program (BPIDP) for our publishing activities. We acknowledge the support of the Canada Council for the Arts for our publishing program. We acknowledge the support of the Government of Ontario through the Ontario Media Development Corporation's Ontario Book Initiative.

Cover illustration: Greg Ruhl

Library and Archives Canada Cataloguing in Publication

Schultz Nicholson, Lorna
     Too many men / Lorna Schultz Nicholson

(Sports stories; 89)

ISBN-13: 978-1-55028-949-7 (bound)
ISBN-10: 1-55028-949-7 (bound)
ISBN-13: 978-1-55028-948-0 (pbk.)
ISBN-10: 1-55028-948-9 (pbk.)
I. Title. II. Series: Sports stories (Toronto, Ont.); 89.

PS8637.C58T66 2006	jC813'6	C2006-903657-8

James Lorimer & Company Ltd.,
Publishers
317 Adelaide St. West
Suite 1002
Toronto, Ontario
M5V 1P9
www.lorimer.ca

Distributed in the United States by:
Orca Book Publishers
P.O. Box 468
Custer, WA USA
98240-0468

Printed and bound in Canada.

CONTENTS

Acknowledgements

I would like to thank every goalie out there. You work so hard in this wonderful game that we all love so much. I have to give a special thanks to Cole Cheveldave, because he sat with me for hours and answered my questions. He allowed me to get a glimpse inside the mind of a goalie and was very patient with each and every question. And I asked a lot. Keep stopping those shots Cole. I know you'll go far!

Of course, as always, I have to thank the Lorimer team, especially my goalies, Hadley Dyer, Jim Lorimer and the Lorimer team, for stoping my shots. (My crazy ideas that get out of hand.) They keep me in the game for sure.

And then there's our wonderful Canadian hockey community that just keeps embracing my books to promote literacy. Thanks to Ian Ellis and Dave Branch of the OHL, Ron Robison and Yvonne Bergmen at the WHL, and everyone at the BCJHL for encouraging young people to read.

And last, (I always save the best for last), I want to thank you, my reader, for telling me to keep writing these books! Please enjoy!

To all Goalies, you're special

1 Minding the Net

Sam Douglas yanked his massive hockey bag filled with goalie equipment off the conveyor belt at the Ottawa airport. Why did it seem to weigh more than usual? He glanced around the strange airport at all the people rushing to pick up bags. They were probably on holidays. His stomach churned. This sure wasn't a vacation for him. He was *moving* to Ottawa.

"Slammer, you have to get more than your hockey equipment." Sam's seventeen-year-old brother Brian snapped his fingers in front of Sam's face. "Wakey, wakey."

Sam scowled and pushed away Brian's arm. "I know." He glared at his brother. "You've only picked up one bag."

Brian crossed his arms across his chest and stared down at Sam. He looked like a giraffe with his skinny arms and neck. "Yeah, but it's a heavy one," said Brian. "And one heavy one is equivalent to two lighter ones.

But how would you know that? Math is not your best subject."

"Why do you have to relate everything to math?" Sam snarled. "You're so lazy when it comes to anything but schoolwork. I bet your new room is a pigsty in two minutes flat. And I bet you can't lift my hockey bag, you skinny weakling."

"Hey," butted in Andy, Sam's oldest brother. At nineteen, he had arms the size of logs from pumping weights and working construction. Sam hoped to look like him one day. Andy easily hoisted a bag onto an airport cart. "Come on you guys. Help, okay?"

"I'm helping, but Brainer isn't." Sam dodged around the crowd and went back to the conveyor belt. Each family member had maxed out on their baggage allowance, and the rest of their belongings were being shipped. When Sam saw a black suitcase with *Douglas* written on the tag, he pulled it off and carried it to their carts.

His mother counted the bags. "I think we have them all," she said.

Sam glanced at Brian. Had he carried only one bag? The guy always got away with doing nothing, and their mom never seemed to notice anything but his brilliant report card.

Mrs. Douglas looked at her watch. "Dad will be outside with the van." Then she attempted to smile. "Well, shall we head to our new home?"

Sam noticed the sad look in his mother's eyes, so he forced a broad smile. A few days ago, he had heard his mom crying with one of her friends, saying she didn't want to leave her friends and the home she'd spent so much time decorating. "The pictures of the house looked good," he said with false enthusiasm. "I can't wait to see my room."

His mother rested her hand on his shoulder. "You're always 'minding the net,' aren't you, Sam? Whether you're on the ice or not." She tousled his hair. "Thank you for thinking of someone other than yourself."

"It's okay," he said. Then he grinned. "Remember our deal, though. I get a puppy. You promised."

She raised her eyebrows and put her arm around Sam. "We will get you a puppy for being such a good sport."

Andy pushed the cart loaded with the most bags. Sam pushed another cart forward through the automatic door and stepped outside into a strange city. What would it be like to play hockey in a new city? He thought about how he'd jumped up and down and hooted and hollered when he found out he had made the AAA Bantam hockey team in Calgary. Even the thought of a puppy didn't settle his queasy stomach.

★ ★ ★

"How do you feel about today?" Sam's father was driving him to his first hockey practice in Ottawa. Sam had a chance to try out for the Kanata Kings.

Sam slouched in his seat. "This team has three goalies. I have to start as *backup* backup. I might not even dress some nights. How do you think I feel?"

"If you play with confidence, you'll be starting in no time." His father signalled the turn to enter the arena parking lot. "It's great that the coach of this team says he'll give you an evaluation. You're lucky. They could have slotted you on a team without taking a look at you."

"What if I don't make it?" Sam refused to look at his father.

"Everything will work out." His father parked and turned off the car engine.

"I already made a good team this year."

"And you can make another team that's just as good."

"You keep saying that," replied Sam, not moving to open the car door. "But you're not the one who might have to sit on the bench."

His father put a hand on Sam's arm. "Sam, you can stop a puck as well as any other goalie your age."

"You don't know that. You haven't seen these guys play." Sam flung open the car door and stepped outside.

A man who introduced himself as Coach Darren met Sam and his father at the door. "Good to meet you, Sam," he said. "I'll take you to the dressing room and introduce you to the other guys."

Sam nodded, but avoided looking at his dad. He followed the coach down the hall and into the dressing room. Unfamiliar faces stared at him. Sam had played on the same team with the same guys since Tyke hockey. In his head he heard the voice of his best friend, Josh Watson: "You'll do great in Ottawa! Show them a thing or too for all of us." Sam wished Josh was here with him now.

"Guys," said the coach. "I'd like to introduce Sam Douglas. He's from Calgary and he's going to practise with us tonight."

Most of the guys mumbled a "hi." Sam immediately looked for an open spot on the bench.

Sandwiched between two players, he dressed in silence. He put his right foot in his long johns, then his left. Next he put on his jock and pants. Although he went right to left with every piece of equipment, he tied his left skate up first. Once his skates were done up, it was time to put on his blue, red, and white pads — his team colours. They had been new last year. He glanced around. They wouldn't match here.

Sam kneeled down and reached behind to cinch the straps. His hands shook as he tried to tighten them. Sweat dripped down his back. He tried to shake off his nervousness. Once his pads were on, he leaned back against the wall, his blocker and catcher resting in his lap, waiting for confirmation that the ice was ready.

Sam turned slightly and saw the face of the guy beside him on the bench. "Hey," the stranger said. "I'm Steven Becker."

"Hey," replied Sam.

"When did you move here?"

"A week ago."

"What team did you come from?"

"A quadrant Triple-A team in Calgary."

"We play Double-A here in Ottawa, but it's the same thing. At least, that's what my dad said."

Sam nodded.

"What school are you at?"

"Kanata Middle School."

"Hey, me too."

The conversation halted when Coach Darren opened the door. The ice was ready. Sam sucked in a deep breath, put on his helmet, and snapped down his cage.

After skating a few laps for warm-up, Coach Darren called everyone in and explained the first drill, a three-on-two. Fortunately, Sam was familiar with the drill. He could do this.

"Kyle and Jerry, I want you in net for this drill," said Coach Darren. "Sam, I'm going to have Coach Ernie take shots on you. Then we'll rotate you in."

Sam headed to the end zone and got into his goalie position. Coach Ernie fired puck after puck at him, and Sam made every effort to stop them. Although he made some saves, he missed lots too. Why was he playing so lousy? His mind was jumping all over the place. What were they looking for? Was he doing as well as the other goalies?

Finally, Coach Darren yelled for the goalies to rotate. Sam entered the net and skated in front to push some of the snow to the side.

Sam batted each goalpost and got into his crouch. He had to focus or he would end up playing in the house league.

The first shot on net was a slick wrist shot to Sam's glove side. He fumbled the puck, but managed to hold on to it. He closed his eyes to feel the puck inside his glove. He sighed in relief. Then he threw the puck to the side.

From his net, Sam saw the three forwards lining up at the far end zone. They circled around until Coach Darren slapped the puck up the ice. The centre picked it up. He skated a few strides with the puck on the end of his stick, then he passed it to the winger along the boards. Sam couldn't see the players' numbers, so he started to memorize the different players by how they taped their sticks or by the colour of their gloves.

The defence in front of Sam moved forward and tried to angle the winger into the boards, but the winger bounced the puck and smoothly skated around the defence. Sam could see that this winger was a slick player with good hands. Sam scanned the entire ice surface. The winger flying toward him could shoot from a bad angle and, if he had a sharp shot, he might hit a corner. Or he could pass to the other winger who was wide open!

Sam prepared for either move. When the guy with the puck made his pass, Sam shuffled across the net to get an angle on the new shooter. The guy fired the puck to the top corner. Sam snapped his hand up and snatched the puck from mid-air. A familiar feeling washed over him. *That* was more like it.

"Nice Hollywood," said the winger who had made the pass. As the player skated up, Sam saw it was Steven. A Hollywood was when a goalie caught a puck by throwing his arm in the air in a big motion. Sam hadn't made the Hollywood save for show; he had just reacted to the speed of the puck. He saw the approval on Steven's face and raised his glove.

By the end of the practice, Sam knew he'd had a better ending than beginning. He hoped the coaches would forget about his shaky start.

Coach Darren bustled into the dressing room. "Guys, listen up." He paused until the room was silent. "I want you here an hour and a half early on Friday for the exhibition game. This will be a good game to work on line combinations." He paused. "Steven, I want you to wear the *C*. I'll pick the *A*s by game time."

One of the other goalies — Sam thought his name

was Kyle — raised his hand. He gave Sam a sidelong look. "What goalies are dressing?" he asked.

"You'll start, Kyle," Coach Darren replied. "Jerry, you'll be on the bench and play the second half. Sam, you start getting a feel for our league by watching from the stands."

Sam hung his head. How degrading. He didn't even get to dress. After the coach left, Sam quickly got out of his equipment. He was rushing through the arena lobby, anxious to get away from everyone, when he heard his name.

"Hey, Sam." It was Steven, running to catch up. Sam didn't want to talk to anyone.

"You made some awesome saves today." Sam noticed that, even before the *C* was on Steven's sweater, he talked like a captain.

"That's not what your coach thinks," replied Sam.

"I know you're not dressing for our game, but stick it out, okay? We may need another goalie. Kyle has a girlfriend who hates hockey."

"So?" said Sam.

"We could use a goalie like you." Steven seemed comfortable speaking for the team.

Sam tilted his head and stared at Steven for a moment. Could he trust this guy? Sam nodded, then turned and walked away.

2 Watching the Play

On game day, Sam dressed in his good pants, white shirt, and tie. It was going to be hard, watching from the sidelines. But even though he wasn't playing, Sam had followed his pre-game ritual. He'd eaten a good lunch, gone for a walk, watched a half hour of television, and visualized being in the net and stopping pucks. Why he went through the process, he wasn't sure, but he did. In a funny way it made him feel part of this strange team.

Sam had e-mailed Josh and told him that he wasn't dressing, and Josh had been shocked. Sam had made the top team every year as the number-one goalie. Now, he wasn't just benched, he was watching from the stands.

Sam didn't talk in the car on the way to the rink. He never did. His dad and mom both knew to be quiet. Once they reached the arena, he told his father he was leaving his equipment in the car.

In the arena lobby, Sam didn't know what to do.

Should he go to the dressing room? And do what? Sit there and watch everyone dress. He decided to watch a bit of the game being played before the Kanata Kings game. The cold air blasted him as he entered the rink area.

He stood by the glass. It looked like a peewee game. Sam focused on the goalie, who was sitting too far back in his net. When a forward from the other team rushed toward the net, Sam whispered to himself, "Move out. Challenge." But the goalie let the puck in on a low wrist shot. The young goalie slapped his stick on the ice. Sam knew how it felt. If Sam, as the goalie, made a mistake, he took on the responsibility for the score.

Sam continued watching. He wanted to get on the ice and give the goalie a few tips. His stomach churned as he thought about not playing tonight. What if this team didn't want him? What if they decided to keep three goalies and he had to do this all the time? What if —

"Sam." Coach Darren tapped him on the shoulder. Sam jumped.

"I didn't mean to startle you," said Coach Darren. "Listen, Kyle just phoned. He isn't coming today." Coach Darren looked away for a minute, obviously not happy with Kyle. When he turned back to Sam, he asked, "Did you bring your equipment?"

"Yes," said Sam.

"I want you to dress." He patted Sam on the back and left.

* * *

Sam dressed in record time. After warm-up, he stood at the end of the bench. He leaned his chin on his hands and watched Jerry prepare his net. The referee blew the whistle and motioned for both teams to take their positions at the face-off.

The game started, and Sam watched Jerry's every move and the entire picture on the ice. Like the pee-wee goalie, Jerry sat too far back in his net.

The other team had a defence with a wicked slap-shot. The teams lined up in the Kings end zone for a face-off. The other team won the face-off and sent the puck back to the defence. He wound up for a slap shot. Sam eyed Jerry. The puck was shot low, and Jerry went down to make a butterfly save. Wow! Sam was amazed at Jerry's butterfly. The guy could get his pads right together. As hard as he tried, Sam knew his pads were always a few inches apart, making his five-hole bigger than Jerry's. He wondered if he would get the chance to work on this part of his game with Jerry.

After the first period the Kings were down 2–0. A slick stick-handler from the other team scored the first two goals of the game by deking Jerry and roofing the puck. Same move both times. Sam thought about how he would try to bounce the puck off his shoulder to make the save, or try to block it by moving his body across the net.

In the dressing room during the first and second period, Sam waited for Coach Darren to say he wanted Sam to play. But he never said anything. So Sam took his position on the bench again. Every few minutes he would look over at Coach Darren to see if he was going to motion for him to go out. When the Kings were down 3–2, Sam was sure he'd get his chance. But he didn't.

Although the Kings fought hard, they ended up losing the game 3–2. Steven scored a goal and picked up an assist.

Sam didn't play.

In the dressing room, Sam said to Steven, "Nice goal."

"Thanks," Steven replied. "Good thing we have boot camp coming up."

"Is that why we don't have any games?" Sam asked. Coach had given Sam's parents a schedule and he found it odd they didn't play a game for weeks.

"Yup." Steven raised his eyebrows. "Coach Darren always does this before our first league game to get us in shape. By the end of it, I get so tired that I even fall asleep at school. It's a good thing nothing is really happening in class yet." Steven yanked his jersey over his head.

Sam leaned over and unlaced his skate. If he proved

himself at boot camp, maybe Coach Darren would let him play. Maybe Steven would talk to him at school and he'd have a friend. Maybe everything would work out okay.

3 On Top of the World

Sam whipped his glove hand in the air to snag the flying puck. He quickly closed his glove once he felt the puck inside. The whistle blew. He tossed the puck on the ice and flipped up his mask to swig some water.

"You really robbed that guy, Hollywood!" Steven swatted Sam's pads with his stick, then skated to his wing.

It felt great to be back in the net during a game! Sam found that boot camp had given him a chance to prove himself and get to know his teammates. Kyle had missed three practices and Coach Darren had given him an ultimatum. So he quit. Now Sam and Jerry were the only goalies on the Kanata Kings.

Sam sucked in a deep breath and snapped his mask down. The score was tied 2–2 with four minutes left in the third period. The pressure was on at the end of this game between the Kanata Kings and their rivals, the Gloucester Chiefs.

Sam crouched, making sure his stick was on the ice. A quick shot off the face-off could be in his net in a flash if his stick wasn't in the right place. He positioned his elbows out to the side of his body to give him better range of motion and so he would look bigger. Today he had to do everything he could to stop the opposition. He had to play well to secure a spot as first goalie.

The Kings lined up. Sam fixed his gaze on the puck in the ref's hand. His heart thumped, but he ignored it. He had to. He couldn't lose sight of the puck. He quickly ran through his stance checklist: glove hand halfway between his knee and hip; blocker outside of his pad and in front; don't hunch, stand straighter … the puck dropped.

The two centres fought for the puck and the Kings' forward won. It landed on a Kings' defenceman, who stick-handled behind the net. But the Chiefs were an aggressive team, and they fore-checked their way into a battle along the boards behind Sam's net. Because he didn't have eyes in the back of his head, Sam had to listen to the sounds and keep his head on a swivel. He had to be ready for a wrap-around.

Sam swung over to the right and held his pad against the post to cut the gap. Which way would the puck come out? Out of the corner of his eye he saw that the Chiefs' forward had Sam's defence pinned. Another player swooped in and pushed the puck.

Sam shuffled to the other side.

Then back again.

Suddenly, Steven flew in from his position on right wing for support, crushing the Chiefs forward in a hit that rattled the glass.

The puck bounced. Sam's left defence picked it up and fired it up the boards to Alex Campbell, the Kings' left winger. But the pass went too long and, although Alex tried, he couldn't get it on the end of his stick. Now a Chiefs' defence had the puck on the blue line. He wound up for a slapshot, and Sam stuck his glove out in preparation. But instead of taking the slapshot, the Chiefs' defence passed it over to his partner on the line. Sam shifted his body, trying to see. Players jostled in front of the net, screening his vision.

The puck was cycled to the corner. Then back out to the defence. Then over to the other defence. He moved in closer to Sam and the net. Who else was open? Sam still couldn't see.

The defence made a cross pass. The winger one-timed it. Sam heard the crack, anticipated the shot. It bounced off his pads. A rebound! Off Sam's pads again.

Then Steven swatted the puck away. Alex picked it up and skated over the blue line and out of the Kings' end. Sam breathed a sigh of relief.

Watching the play from his end Sam saw Alex shoot the puck into Gloucester's end zone so the Kings could make a line change. Steven was headed into the players bench, and the other Kings' forward had stepped onto the ice, when a Gloucester player smacked the puck and it hit Steven's stick. The whistle shrilled.

Penalty: too many men.

Coach Darren shook his head and looked to the clock. There were only forty seconds left to play in the third period.

Sam's throat clogged. His heart raced. He lifted his mask and gulped down some water. With the Kings a man short, the play most likely would be in his end, and the Chiefs would be rapid-firing the puck at him. The ref motioned for the face-off to take place inside the Kanata end. Sam's nerves tingled. Sweat beaded on his forehead. He had to stay focused. It was up to him. He took his stance.

The puck dropped.

A Chiefs' defence took possession on the blue line. The puck went over to the other defence. And back. Then it went down to the winger, who held on to it while looking for an open man. The Kings' defence swatted at the puck, trying to intercept a pass. No go. The puck went back to the blue line again.

Players bumped in front of Sam, stick against stick, body against body.

"Cover the winger," yelled Sam. The guy was wide open.

The defence nailed a pass to the open man who one-timed it. Sam threw out his blocker hand. The puck nipped the corner and landed out front. Sam fell on the puck. Players from both teams landed on top of him.

The ref and linesmen screeched to the huddle, spraying snow, pulling guys off Sam, trying to stop the roughing in front. Sam adjusted his mask. He glanced at the clock. Twenty seconds left.

Again the face-off was in his end. The puck went back to the line. But the defence for the Chiefs made a slip and fumbled with the puck. Steven charged forward.

"Go!" yelled the crowd.

Steven broke open.

"All the way!" yelled Coach Darren.

Steven skated hard toward the Gloucester goalie. Close to the net, he deked and roofed the puck into the top corner!

The Kings threw their gloves in the air and raced toward Sam. Grinning, he braced himself for the dog-pile, knowing he would be on the bottom.

The Kings had beaten the Chiefs 3–2.

★ ★ ★

"Great game, Sam," said Steven's dad in the Gloucester arena lobby.

"Thanks." Sam beamed. When his team won, he felt great, on top of the world. If they lost … well, he tried to figure out why he had let in the goals.

"That was a good intense game," said Mr. Douglas, patting Sam on the back. "You play against Cumberland next."

Mr. Douglas turned to Steven and patted him on the back too. "That was quite the goal at the end."

"He roofed it," said Sam. "You gotta love those."

Steven bobbed his head. "I can't wait to play Cumberland. Remember last year, Sam …" He paused to shake his head. "I keep forgetting you weren't here last year."

In just a couple of weeks, Sam and Steven had become friends. They went to the same school and sometimes ate lunch together. Steven was happy that Sam had moved because he was a great addition to their team.

"I hope we win provincials this year," said Steven. He playfully punched Sam on the arm. "With you on our team, we've got a good chance at being All-Ontario Champs!"

Sam smiled. "Thanks," he said. Sam had worked hard during the boot camp to prove himself. He had been thrilled when Coach had given him the opportunity to play this important game.

Steven high-fived Sam and both boys grinned.

"Well," said Sam's mother. "I hate to break up this enthusiasm for winning but…" she glanced at her watch, "we should get going. It will take an hour to get home, what with the traffic and the Senators game just ending. Both your brothers are going out tonight, Sam. Andy is working. Brian is at the library studying, then he's playing pickup hockey at midnight. They're leaving Molly in her kennel. I don't want her to be alone for too long."

"I haven't seen your new puppy yet," said Steven to Sam.

"She's about this big." Sam held out his hand with the palm up. When they had gone to choose a puppy to reward Sam for accepting the move to Ottawa, he had fallen in love with tiny white Molly and her black ears. Having her had made the first weeks in the new city bearable for Sam.

"And at that size her bladder doesn't hold much," said Mrs. Douglas. "We really should head out."

"I'm starving," said Sam.

"We don't have much time to stop," replied his father. "Maybe we can hit a drive-through."

"Hey, I've got an idea," said Steven. He turned to his parents. "Why don't we take Sam, since we were going to stop to eat anyway? Then when we drop him off, I can see the puppy."

"Maybe you can sleep over too," said Sam. "We don't have a game tomorrow, just practice."

Mr. Becker shrugged. "You might as well take advantage of tonight. It will be the last opportunity for a few weekends. You have a pretty busy schedule coming up."

"So, can Steven sleep over?" Sam asked his parents.

Mr. Douglas turned to Mrs. Douglas. "What do you think?"

She looked at Sam with a twinkle in her eye. "I guess so." She had a funny little curl to her lip. "Are you going to get up early to take the puppy out, Sam?"

Sam looked at Steven then looked back at his mom. "Can't you do it this once? Steven and I will need our beauty rest. Right, Steven?"

"I don't mind getting up to take the dog out, Hollywood," said Steven, using the nickname he had given Sam in boot camp. "But you might need that beauty sleep."

Sam shook his head and waved his friend closer. Then he cupped his hands and whispered in Steven's ear, "She gets up at six in the morning."

"That early?" groaned Steven.

"Yes, that early," said Mrs. Douglas. She jokingly frowned at Sam. "I like the comment about 'just this once.'"

"What?" Sam frowned back at his mother.

"Sam, you've only ever taken the dog out once."

"And she's your dog." Mr. Douglas piped into the conversation. "You promised you'd handle her. We've got enough stress just trying to get the boxes unpacked."

"Come on, Dad. Stay out of this okay? It's between Mom and me." Sam held up his hand. "Please, Mom."

"All right. I'll get up with the dog."

"Thanks, Mom, you're the best."

"Yeah, okay. Stop trying to butter me up. You'll be on morning duty for the rest of the week, hockey or no hockey." Mrs. Douglas raised her eyebrows at Sam.

"I know, I know," said Sam.

Mr. Douglas turned to Sam. "We'll take your equipment."

"Awesome." Sam handed his father his big goalie bag and sheepishly gave his stick to his mother, who gave him the raised-eyebrows look again.

"So now I'm your stick boy too," she said. "You take this being-the-youngest too far sometimes. Shaking her head, she held out her hand for Sam's stick. "What would you do without me?"

"Thanks, Mom." Sam smiled a fake grin that made his face look like a half-moon. "I'll see you at home."

4 An Unlucky Break

The lights were off in Sam's house when Mr. Becker pulled up front. Both boys jumped out of the car and raced up the sidewalk.

"It doesn't look like anyone's home," said Steven.

"My parents probably went to bed," said Sam. "Sometimes my dad is in bed by nine on a Saturday night. How boring is that?"

Sam tried to push open the front door but it was locked. He banged on the door as hard as he could. No answer.

"They could have waited up for me," he said as he bent to get the spare key hidden under a hedgehog shoe cleaner.

As soon as he opened the door, he flipped on the light and yelled out, "Mom, Dad!"

There was no answer. Sam heard the puppy whimpering. "She's in her kennel," he said. "They must have gone to bed. What a bunch of old fogies."

Sam and Steven ran to the mud room. Now Molly was yelping and scratching at the bars in her kennel. Sam opened up the kennel and took the puppy out, showing her to Steven. "I like her black ears best."

"Let me hold her," said Steven.

As Sam passed Molly to Steven's outstretched hands, she wagged her tail and started to piddle.

"Gross!" said Sam. "She's peeing all over my hand!"

Laughing, Steven backed up. "I don't want to hold her now."

"She shouldn't have to go to the bathroom already. My mom would have let her out when she came home. Mom!" Sam placed Molly on the floor and she immediately squatted, leaving a big yellow puddle on the tiled floor.

"Whoa," said Steven. "That's a huge puddle for such a small dog. We better take her outside."

"Too late. She's already gone." Sam pointed to the ground. "Take care of her for a sec, okay? I'm going to see my mom."

Steven looked at Sam wide-eyed. "Shouldn't we, like, clean this up or something?"

Sam looked around the mud room, which doubled as a laundry room, spotted a dirty towel in the laundry hamper, and threw it at Steven. "Use this," he said, ignoring the grimace on his friend's face.

Then he ran up the stairs to the master bedroom at

31

the end of the hall. He knocked on the door. "Mom, Dad," he said.

No answer.

"Mom, Dad," he said again. When there was still no answer, he pushed open the door and saw the empty, made bed. "Where are they?" he said to himself.

Totally confused, Sam sped down the stairs two at a time. He was running through the kitchen to the mud room when the phone rang. He screeched to a stop and picked up the cordless. "Hello," he blurted.

"Sam, it's Dad."

"Where are you?"

"At the Ottawa General Hospital."

"Hospital? Why are you at the hospital?" Steven had joined Sam in the kitchen, and was holding the puppy, stroking her ears.

"Don't worry, Sam," continued his Dad. "We were in a little accident on the way home but we're both going to be okay."

"Accident?!"

"Yeah, someone side-swiped us on the highway and we had to veer off the road. I'm perfectly fine but … your mom has broken her leg. They're resetting it now. And they'll have to cast it too. Our car is totalled, but I phoned Andy at work to come pick us up. Your mom is adamant about not staying in the hospital any longer than she has too."

"How bad is she hurt?"

"It's a bad break. We're both a bit bruised too. But Andy's on his way now. Is Steven still there?"

"Yeah," said Sam. "Why didn't you call earlier?"

"I tried Steven's dad on his cell and left a message. He must have it turned off. Is Brian home yet?"

Sam played with a pencil that was on the kitchen counter. His stomach felt sick as he watched the pencil twirl.

"You still there, Sam?" His dad asked.

"Brian's not home yet." Sam let the pencil come to a stop.

"I want you to go to Steven's for the night. I'll call his dad as soon as I hang up with you. I don't want you alone. Brian was on the ice at midnight. I haven't been able to reach him. And we're going to be a few hours yet."

"I can wait here by myself. When I broke my arm, they cast it right away."

"Sam, your mom broke her femur, her thigh. This is not a little break. It could take a while for them to finish what they have to do."

"You said she was okay."

"She is. The injury is not life-threatening. We're lucky Sam. Really lucky. The doctors said she'll be just fine if she gets lots of rest."

★ ★ ★

Sam slept over at Steven's house, but he didn't really sleep. All night he lay awake, thinking about his mother with a broken leg. Would she have to use crutches? Or maybe a wheelchair? He just couldn't picture his mother with a cast on her leg. He saw the clock read 3:00 before he fell asleep.

When he awoke, the room was still dark. He sat up and looked at the clock radio, which read 7:00. He'd slept for only four hours. Sam stared at the ceiling wondering what to do. He didn't know the Becker's that well and had only slept over Steven's house once before. Steven snored beside him.

Sam had brought Molly with him to Steven's, not wanting to leave her alone. Before they went to bed he'd put her in her kennel and left her in the Becker's mud room. Now Sam wanted to see her.

He kept staring at the clock. After another half hour, he poked Steven.

"You awake?"

"No," said Steven rolling over. "It's only seven-thirty."

Steven's breath slowed again and Sam knew he'd fallen back to sleep. There was no way Sam could stay in bed any longer. He tiptoed down the stairs and slowly entered the kitchen. Mr. Becker sat at the kitchen table with the Sunday morning newspaper, sipping a cup of coffee. Molly was also up and playing with an old tennis ball. When Molly saw Sam, she bounded over to him.

"Hey, Sam." Mr. Becker placed his newspaper on the table. "You're up early."

"Has she been out yet?" Sam bent over and picked up Molly.

"She has. She's an early riser. I heard her whining, and since I was already awake, I thought I'd take her out and let you boys sleep."

"Thanks," said Sam shyly. "Sometimes my mom does that too."

"Sometimes." Mr. Becker winked at Sam.

Sam smiled. "She says I need my rest for hockey." He paused, unsure of how to ask the next question.

Finally he blurted out, "Can you drive me home?"

Mr. Becker stood and put his hand on Sam's shoulder. "Sure," he said in an understanding tone. "But I'm not sure anyone will be up though. I talked to your dad last night after you went to bed and he thought your mom would be released from the hospital around six in the morning."

"Six? That's crazy. She just broke her leg."

"I think you should be prepared," said Mr. Becker. "From what your dad told me, your mom will need total bed rest for a while."

★ ★ ★

The lights were off at Sam's house when Mr. Becker dropped him off. Sam cradled Molly in his arm and carried the kennel with his free hand. He entered the house, put the kennel down, and immediately headed upstairs to his parents' bedroom. Molly licked his face.

Only his dad slept in the king-sized bed. "Dad." Sam gently shook his father's shoulders. A knot formed in Sam's stomach. Where was his mom? Mr. Becker said she had been released, didn't he? Sam wanted her to be at home not in the hospital.

"Sam." His dad sat up and ran his hand through his rumpled hair. "What time is it?" His voice was groggy.

"Eight-fifteen."

"You're up early. And I'm sleeping late." He pressed his fingers to his brow. "After eight already, eh?" Sam's dad was an early riser, always up by seven.

"Where's Mom?"

"She can't climb the stairs, so she's sleeping in the spare room. It's better down there because of the adjoining bathroom."

"Do you think I can see her?"

"They gave her a lot of painkillers. But once she's awake she'd love to see you. She'll probably be a bit out of it for a few days, though."

Sam sat on the end of the bed.

"We're going to have to manage without her," said his dad. "Everyone will have to help with the cooking and I'll have to get Brian to drive you to hockey when Andy and I are working. The doctors said she has to stay off her feet for at least a week. No pressure on the leg at all."

"I can help around the house too," said Sam bravely. "I know how to make Kraft Dinner."

★ ★ ★

"Hey, Mom."

Sam tiptoed into the spare room with Molly in his arms. Finally, his mother was awake. He had been listening outside the door for over an hour, waiting to hear her stir. It was just eleven in the morning, but Sam felt as if he'd been up forever. Andy and Brian were still sleeping.

Sam stared at his mom's cast. It went all the way from her ankle right up to her hip. "Wow," he said. "That's a huge cast."

"Sam, sweetie." She tried to smile but ended up grimacing when she moved to sit up. She patted the end of the bed. "How's our Molly?"

"Good," said Sam. There was no way he was going to tell his mother that in the last three hours she'd peed twice in the house and gone poo once. "That's the biggest cast I've ever seen." He handed the puppy to her. Molly jumped and bounced and started playing tug-of-war with the bedcovers.

"You want to be the first to sign it?"

"Sure! I'll go get a marker."

When Sam went into the kitchen Andy was standing in front of the refrigerator slugging back orange juice from the container, his biceps bulging from tilting the carton.

"I'm going to be the first to sign Mom's cast." Sam rifled through the junk drawer looking, for a permanent marker.

"Cool." Andy's voice had that half-asleep, scratchy sound. He wiped his mouth and put the orange juice back in the fridge, closing the door with his foot. "When did she wake up?"

"A few minutes ago." Sam tossed scissors, tape, and some pencils from the drawer onto the counter. "I can't find a marker." He pulled out a handful of pens and tossed them on the counter too. "I'll have to ask Mom where one is."

"I don't want you bothering your mother." Mr. Douglas had entered the kitchen. "I need to talk to you boys. Is Brian up?"

"Yeah, I'm up." Brian loped into the room, his head almost hitting the top of the door frame. He yawned and stretched, his limbs looking like the strings on a mop. "How's Mom?" he asked.

"She is going to need our help," said Mr. Douglas, eyeing each boy. "I am counting on you boys to keep the house running smoothly."

"No problem," said Andy. He turned to Sam. "Sammer the Slammer, you're on dish duty."

"Dishes? I don't want to be on dishes." Sam frowned at his brother. Just because they were older, they were always picking on him. Sam often wished he had a younger brother, or at least someone closer to his age.

"Okay," said Brian, wrestling Sam into a headlock. "Then how about laundry? Dirty socks. Gross gaunch." He rubbed Sam's scalp with his knuckles.

"Dad, tell him to stop," Sam squealed as he tried to squirm out of the headlock.

"Guys, guys," said Mr. Douglas, breaking up Brian and Sam. "This is serious. Mother needs our help."

"We're just kidding. We'll work together," said Brian. "I'll make breakfast. How's that?"

"Mom likes poached eggs," said Sam.

"Okay, Slammer." Brian high-fived Sam. "I'll make the eggs, you make the toast."

"And I'll make fruit smoothies," said Andy.

"No protein powder," said Mr. Douglas. "Your mother doesn't like the taste of that stuff."

"Right–o," replied Andy.

5 Minding the House

Breakfast turned out great. And Sam was thrilled when dad said he could take the plate of food in to his mother. Proudly, Sam carried a tray into the room. He had even put a fake flower in a vase. Molly was curled up beside Mom, fast asleep.

"Hi, Mom. Are you hungry?"

She smiled weakly. "A little."

"I hope you like what we made. Brian made the eggs. But I made the toast."

"You're good to me." She glanced down at her cast. By now all the boys had been in to see Mom and had signed it. Andy had drawn a happy face, Brian had written in scrolled letters, and Sam had printed, "*I love you, get well soon!*" and drawn a goalie stick. They had needed her to tell them where the marker was.

Sam watched her pick at her food.

"Don't you like what we made?" he asked.

"Of course," she replied. "My stomach's a bit queasy, that's all." She nibbled on the toast.

"Oh, okay."

After a few more bites, she leaned back against her pillow. Sam had never seen his mother look so tired. Her eyes were rimmed with a funny purple colour and her lips looked dried and chapped. She had bruises on her arms and one on her cheek.

Mom always looked good to Sam, but not today. Normally, when she wasn't working, she bustled about the kitchen, cooking and cleaning. Every once in a while, when she had a cold or the flu, she stayed in bed, but those days were rare. This was definitely the sickest she'd ever been. Mom rolled her head to look at him. "Do you have practice today?"

He nodded. "Later tonight. Eight o'clock, I think."

"When's your next game?"

What a strange question for his mother to ask. She always knew when he played. His mom was his biggest fan. She even had a sweatshirt that said *Hockey Mom*. "Tuesday," he said quietly.

"Oh, that's right." She reached out and he put his hand in hers. He sat on the end of the bed, holding her hand, staring at her. She slowly closed her eyes.

Sam wondered about the rest of his schedule. Mom had everything written out and she was the one who knew when everything took place. Dad always called her the generator, the machine that kept everything moving. When they had arrived in Ottawa, she'd had the boxes unpacked and things put away in less than two weeks. She'd organized Sam and Brian into their new schools and even signed up to help with Sam's hockey team as the Phone Parent. She had decided she would take some time off and not go back to work right away, so she'd joined a gym and bought paint to "freshen up" some rooms. Now she wouldn't be able to paint or work out for a while. She opened her eyes and patted his hand.

"Does Dad have my schedule?" Sam asked.

"It's by the telephone."

"Okay." Sam tried to sound chipper. He didn't want her worrying about hockey schedules.

"This will be the first game I've missed in a long time. I don't know how this happened." She sighed. "How am I going to get the house done if I'm in this bed?"

"Don't worry about any of that stuff. The house looks great just the way it is." Sam stood and picked up the tray of food. "We're going to take care of everything around here."

The corners of her mouth lifted in a small smile. "I've got such great boys. I feel so lucky." Her words slurred a bit and her eyelids drooped. "I think I'm going to rest," she said. "Maybe you should take Molly in case she wakes up before me and has to go outside."

Sam turned off the light when he left the room. In

the kitchen, he plunked the tray on the counter beside the other dirty breakfast dishes. Then he set Molly on the floor. Immediately, she peed. Sam groaned.

Dad sat at the kitchen table reading the newspaper. "Get a paper towel and clean it up. She's your responsibility."

Sam yanked a paper towel off the rack and sopped up the yellow mess. "Gross," he said throwing it in the garbage.

"I thought Brian was supposed to do the dishes," said Sam.

His father peered over his glasses. "He was. He had to go to the library to tutor someone."

"So."

"Sam, Brian makes money tutoring. This is his job. You know how hard he works in school and how badly he wants to be a dentist. Every little bit helps."

"Where's Andy then?" Sam really didn't want to be saddled with the dishes. Trust Brian to find a way out of doing the work at home.

"He's working." Dad folded his newspaper in half and stood up. "I wanted to be home with your mother, so I needed him at the construction site. I'll help you. If both of us work, we'll have it done in no time. Then we'll throw in a load of laundry."

Sam worked hard around the house all day. When it was time for his practice, he was exhausted. Late in the afternoon, he went with his dad to get the rented car they had to use until they got a new car. Mr. Douglas took Sam to the junkyard to take a look at their old car. It looked like an accordion, all folded together.

Brian drove Sam to practice so Dad could stay home with Mom. Everyone in the dressing room asked questions about the accident.

"Did they really total the car?"

"Yeah," said Sam. "They hit a fence post. You should see it. It's crunched." Sam described the state of the car in detail. He was still getting used to the guys on this team, and liked having them hanging on every word.

"How's your Mom?" said Steven.

Sam stood up. "Her cast is this big." He pointed to his hip.

"Really?" said Alex. "Can she walk?"

Sam shook his head. "She can't do anything right now. Maybe in a few days she'll be able to get up. Right now, she even has to use a bedpan."

"A bedpan?!" Steven made a funny face. "Who empties it?"

"My dad."

★ ★ ★

In warm-up, Sam barely made any saves. He'd throw up his glove and miss the puck. Coach Darren didn't seem to notice, as he was too busy writing drills on the white-board. Jerry warmed up at the other end.

Sam was thankful when Coach Darren finally blew the whistle to get the practice started. He skated over to the bench.

"Okay, guys," said Coach Darren, "first drill will be a three-on-two. I want to work on our offence today. When we played Gloucester, I thought our defence looked good. If we play the same defensive game but step up our offence, we'll be way ahead. We need to be drive to the net for every rebound. They have a big goalie and he stands tall in the net, so you will want to keep your shots on the ice. He's got a big five-hole."

Coach Darren paused before he looked at Sam and Jerry. "For today's practice, I want goalies to alternate. Sam, you start in net. Jerry, you go to the far end and work with Coach Ernie. We'll switch you up later."

Coach Darren blew his whistle and everyone hustled to their start positions. The wingers lined up at the far end with the pucks, with the defence just in front of the blue line. Sam skated to his net. Stopping low shots was his strength.

Steven sped down his wing, looking for the pass. Sam glanced briefly at him, then scanned the rest of the ice. He had to know where every player was. If he didn't keep track he could get skunked.

Sam watched Alex gracefully stick-handle down the ice, moving from his centre position to the outside.

The defence tried to stop him, but Alex weaved around him. Convinced Alex would come in and try to score, Sam got ready.

Jordie, on left wing, crossed behind Alex. Alex drop-passed the puck. Sam anticipated a shot from Jordie, but he passed it to Steven. Sam slid across his crease. He'd forgotten about Steven!

Steven one-timed the puck. Sam sunk into splits, trying to stop the shot that was heading to the far corner. His skate nicked it, but it still cruised over the line.

Sam shook his head. How had he let that one in?

In the next ten plays, Sam stopped only one out of ten shots.

Finally, the whistle blew to change up the goalies. Sam skated to the bench, swigged some water, and skated to the far end of the rink where Coach Ernie had the pucks lined up.

"Whenever you're ready, Sam," said Coach Ernie.

Sam nodded and got into position. Coach Ernie fired the pucks one after the other. The drill was to help increase Sam's reaction time. Sam kept throwing his glove up, shifting his blocker, skating from side to side. When Coach Ernie had finished shooting all the pucks, Sam turned to see most of them in the net. He'd made only one save. He felt like his blood was boiling. He batted the pucks out.

Then he talked to himself. "Come on, Sam. You can do it. Watch the puck. Hang on to it. Freeze it."

Once again Coach Ernie lined up the pucks. "This time, snap shots," he said.

Sam nodded. He saved the first one. And the second. And the third. But then his vision became fuzzy and he lost sight of the puck. Four went in. Then five. Then six. Luckily he managed to block the last two with his body.

They did the drill four more times, and each time Sam let in more than he saved. Sam couldn't believe it. Usually, it was the other way around.

Coach Ernie skated over to Sam. "Your reaction time is off."

"I know," said Sam.

Coach Ernie patted him on the back. "I heard you had a tough night last night. Go get some water."

With five minutes left in the practice, Coach Darren called everyone in to recap the practice. Coach Ernie was setting up both nets in the far end of the rink. While Sam listened to Coach Darren, he also glanced at Coach Ernie. With the nets like that they were going to end practice with his favourite relay game.

Coach Darren smiled. "Good work, guys. Now it's time for some fun." He numbered everyone, putting them into two groups. "Sam, you're with group one; Jerry, you're group two."

Steven skated beside Sam. "Awesome," he said. "I'm shooting on Jerry this time. When I shoot on you, you always make too many saves and my team doesn't win."

Sam grinned. He loved making save after save, especially on guys like Alex who got frustrated. Sometimes Sam would even smack the puck all the way down the ice so the shooter would have to skate after it.

Sam got in his net. He was ready.

The whistle blew. Alex was Sam's first shooter. He raced to get his puck. All the guys cheered their teammates from the sidelines. Sam anticipated Alex's deke and threw his glove in the air. The puck zinged by him. Alex pumped his arm and skated to the end so the next guy on his team could go. This time, Sam made the first save, but missed the rebound. What was wrong with him? Out of the corner of his eye, Sam could see that Jerry was still making saves on his first player.

When Sam was down to his last player, Jerry still had three more to go. Sam had to make saves. And lots of them. He saved the first shot, batting the puck to the corner. He could hear the cheers. Did Jerry just make a save or let one in?

Another shot was fired, aimed to his glove. Sam made the save and threw the puck as far as he could. Again he heard cheering. He snatched a glance to see what was happening on the other side. Yes, Jerry was down to one player too!

Suddenly, Sam saw Jordie coming in on him. "Shoot," yelled Jordie's teammates sitting on the ice, waving their arms, hoping to be victorious. Sam got ready for the low shot. But Jordie deked. Sam reached his stick out, hoping to stick check the puck. But Jordie slid the puck over and snapped it in the top corner.

"Yeah, we won!" Alex yelled.

Sam sucked in a deep breath. He'd never lost at this game.

"Great job, Jerry," said Coach Darren. "You made some amazing saves."

Sam skated directly to the dressing room.

"Shake it off," whispered Steven to Sam when they were getting undressed. "It's one practice."

"Doesn't matter," said Sam. "I sucked out there today."

6 Waking Up Too Early

Sam could hardly carry his bag from the garage into the mud room.

"How was practice?" Dad stood in the doorway.

"Good." Sam pulled out his chest pad and put it on a hook. He didn't want his family to know how lousy he'd played in practice. No one needed to listen to his whining.

"Your dog peed three times while you were gone," yelled Andy from the kitchen.

Sam finished spreading his equipment out to dry, then went into the kitchen. Only a few dishes sat on the counter. It wasn't spotless but it looked fine. Dad probably cleaned up. Sam opened the fridge.

"Did you hear me? Your dog —"

"I heard you. Why didn't you take her out?"

"I did," replied Andy. "But she doesn't go, then she comes inside and goes."

Sam sighed. Even though she was Sam's dog, Mom

usually took her out. "You have to stay with her until she goes," he repeated what Mom had told him.

"Well, you're in charge now. She's your dog."

Molly began her high-pitched whining at 6:00 a.m. Sam groaned and rolled over. He'd decided to keep her kennel in his room so Mom wouldn't hear her in the morning and wake up.

"Go back to sleep," he said. But she kept whining.

Finally, he got up and opened her kennel door. She came bounding out, wagging her tail so hard her entire body shook. Rubbing his eyes, Sam glanced around his room for a hoodie. He found one underneath a mound of clothes. Tomorrow, he would have to take these clothes to the laundry room for Mom … Suddenly Sam remembered that his mother couldn't do the laundry. He shoved the clothes under his bed.

Sam picked up Molly and carried her to the back door. The cold air blasted his face when he stepped outside. The temperature had dropped overnight. He shivered. The cold reminded him of Calgary. Molly shivered too. She looked up at him with an, "I'm cold, can we go in?"

"Go to the bathroom," he said. She looked up at him and whined. Sam scratched his head. Had she gone already? He hadn't seen her go. She pawed his leg. Freezing, he picked her up and took her back into the house.

Back in his room, he saw the yellow spot on the carpet. In his sleepy head, he heard his mom's voice: "Sam, you have to carry her to the back door. She'll pee as soon as she's let out of the kennel." Darn, she must have gone while he was searching for a hoodie.

Too tired to clean up the mess, Sam crawled back into bed and curled under the covers. Molly slept on his pillow.

Minutes later, or so it seemed, he heard a loud rap on his door. "Sam, time to get up." His clock read 7:00. Why was Dad waking him up so early?

"Mom never wakes me up until seven-fifteen," he growled.

"Sam, I want you up now. I need to talk to you and your brothers this morning."

"Why?"

"Don't ask questions."

Sam flung the covers off his bed and stomped to the bathroom.

Andy and Brian were already in the kitchen, eating cereal. Brian tipped his bowl and slurped the remaining milk. Then he picked up the box and dumped more cereal into the bowl.

"That's it for the milk," he said, pouring the rest onto his cereal.

"What am I supposed to have?" Sam was cranky. He still didn't understand why his father wouldn't let him sleep for fifteen more minutes.

"Toast," said Andy. "That's what I'm having. I'll pop a few in for you."

"Thanks," mumbled Sam.

"Boys, I have something to talk to you about." Mr. Douglas cleared his throat. Sam glanced at him. He looked so serious. Was something wrong with Mom?

"I have to go to Quebec for some extremely important business meetings," he continued. "I tried to get out of it, but if I don't go, I could lose this condo contract." Sam knew that Dad had been waiting for this go-ahead meeting.

"I know the timing is terrible. Your mother needs my help. They want me there for the week to go over plans." He turned to Andy. "I need you to help manage things here at the Ottawa site while I'm gone."

"I can handle that," said Andy with manly confidence.

Dad looked at Sam and Brian. "What if I called Aunt Sharon to come in and help you boys, since Andy is going to be busy?" He ran his hand through his hair, a gesture that showed Sam he was stressed. "She could possibly drive in from Toronto and look after things."

Sam and Brian exchanged looks. Aunt Sharon was super bossy, and having Dad's sister around would just make things worse.

"Dad, we'll be fine," said Brian. "I can drive. And Sam and I can help around the house."

"Are you sure?" Mr. Douglas didn't seem convinced. "What about your mother during the day?"

"I have an idea," piped up Sam, suddenly feeling much better about the situation. "I'll stay home from school."

"Nice try, Slammer," said Andy, jabbing him on the shoulder. Sam ducked and jabbed Andy back.

Dad looked at Sam. "I'd like you to walk home at lunch and make something for your mother to eat."

"I can do that," said Sam.

Then Dad looked at Brian. "I want you to organize breakfast, and I want you to come home after school and make dinner." He paused to glance from Brian to Sam, then back to Brian. "Share breakfast responsibilities and the housework. Sam, if Brian cooks dinner, your responsibility will be the dishes." Then he turned to Andy. "I know you don't have time to do the household stuff because you'll be working a lot. These boys can handle the house."

"What about my hockey?" Sam asked.

Again Mr. Douglas ran his hand through his hair. "Brian can take you. And if he gets too busy, you can phone the Beckers."

"Sounds cool to me," said Brian.

Still thinking about everything, Mr. Douglas nodded his head. "Okay. Does everyone know their roles?"

The boys nodded.

"I talked with your mom this morning. She knows

how important it is for me to attend this meeting. The good news is that she actually was able to get up this morning and go to the bathroom." He paused to breathe. After he blew out a gush of air, he said, "But that's all she can do."

"We'll be fine at home, Dad," said Andy. Then he patted his father on the back. "And I'll make you proud at work."

Dad smiled and nodded his head. "Thanks, guys."

Brian patted his father on the back. "Don't worry about anything, Dad. We're cool."

Sam glanced around the kitchen. The milk jug was empty. Dishes were piled on the counter. Cereal littered the table.

And a brown clump of puppy poo sat under the table.

7 Home for Lunch

Sam cleaned up Molly's mess, stuffed an apple and granola bar in his coat pocket, and shoved his books in his backpack. Then he went in to see his mother. She was already sitting propped up, four pillows behind her back.

"Hi," he said. "How are you feeling today?"

"Better. You ready for school?" She smiled. She did look better. Her cheeks had a pink tinge.

"Yup."

"Did you get your homework done?"

"Yup." With all the commotion over the weekend, Sam had forgotten to write a response for English class. "I'll come home at lunch today, okay?"

"You don't have to. I'll be fine by myself, you know." She winked. "Your dad worries way too much."

"But I want to. It's the deal I made with Dad. He said the doctors said you can't put any weight on your leg for at least five days."

She sipped some water from a glass on the night table.

"He's right," she said. "The doctors did say that. But I'm only on my second day, and I'm already going crazy." She pointed to a pile of books and a stack of magazines beside her bed. "I'll catch up on my reading."

"I'll make your lunch," said Sam. "You can't go to the kitchen. Dad said you can only get up to go to the bathroom."

"You father really listened to those doctors." She reached out to touch his cheek. "I look forward to seeing you, but only if it doesn't conflict with anything at school."

Sam was halfway to school when he remembered he forgot to put Molly in her kennel. *Oops.* He hoped she wouldn't chew anything. Or go to the bathroom again. He picked up his pace. The dampness of the dreary day sunk right to his bones. Sam yanked up the collar on his coat to cover his stinging ears.

Once inside the school, Sam slowed down. To Sam, his new school was like one big gigantic maze. His first week, he'd gotten lost at least ten times.

He glanced at his watch and noted that he had only five minutes until the bell rang. With his head down, he barrelled down the hall. He jostled into a few students but didn't look at them, he just kept walking. The only people he knew were a few guys on his team who also went to this school.

He walked down one hall, then another, before he rounded the corner to get to his locker. When he saw Steven and a girl named Erica standing by his locker, he breathed a sigh of relief. Finally, someone he knew. Steven and Erica were always together at school.

"Hey, Sam. How's your mom?" Erica's reddish eyebrows were squished together, and she looked serious and honestly concerned. Erica and Steven had been friends for years. She played volleyball and basketball, and Sam had gone to a couple of her games with Steven. She reminded Sam of Kaleigh, a girl he had played hockey with in Calgary. They were both friendly, athletic, and pretty, but Erica had red hair and Kaleigh's was blonde.

"She's a bit better today," replied Sam. "But she still has to stay in bed. She can't put pressure on the leg for at least five days or it might not heal properly." He tried to think about what he had first period. His mind blurred.

"Wow." Erica's eyes opened wide. "She must have a real bad break."

"It's her femur. Her leg went through the front of the car. I have to go home at lunch to take care of her." He pushed his eyebrows together. "We have math first, right?"

"Yeah." Erica giggled. "We've had math first period on Monday since you got to this school. Hey, did you forget, we have that tutorial for math at lunch today? I guess that mid term we have on Friday is going to be a killer. This is the hardest unit."

Sam groaned. "I can't go. I'll have to tell the teachers." He paused. "My dad had to go out of town and I'm in charge of making lunch for my mom."

"I think that's great," said Erica. "No teacher will get mad at you for that."

Erica's comment made Sam think about the English response he hadn't done. Bonus. He'd go to his English teacher and tell her why he didn't get it done. Erica was right. Every teacher would understand, especially since he was the new kid at school.

"I printed off our hockey schedule," said Steven.

Sam scanned the list. "Can we beat all these teams?"

"We can beat Cumberland for sure. And Nepean isn't that great this year. Neither is West Carlton. But Perth is good, and so is Orleans," said Steven.

Suddenly, the bell rang. Steven thrust the paper back in his binder.

Sam took his seat at the back of the class. As he listened to the teacher drone on and on, his eyelids became heavy. Every few minutes he jolted upright, trying to keep awake. Finally, he couldn't take it any more and he put his head down on his desk. Suddenly, he felt a jab.

"Sam!" Steven whispered. "Stop snoring."

Dazed, Sam looked at Steven. "I wasn't snoring. Was I?"

"You sound like a truck with no muffler."

When the period finally ended, Sam knew he hadn't heard a word the teacher had said.

Out in the hallway, Erica scrunched up her face. "I don't know why Mr. Lewis always has to give so much homework. It's like he thinks we don't have anything to do but math."

"And we have practice tonight too," said Steven.

"Right," replied Sam. When was he going to get his math done?

★ ★ ★

Sam ran home at lunch. Big raindrops fell from the sky. He flew in the house, shaking his hair, to find Molly sitting on the sofa in the living room, tangled up in a pile of chewed papers. She wagged her tail and whined, obviously happy to see him. How did she get on the good sofa?

"What are you chewing?" he asked the puppy, whispering so his mother wouldn't hear.

Sam picked up the soggy papers. "Gross." He crumpled them into a ball.

Had Molly done any other damage? Sam glanced around the room. Everything seemed okay, except for the small brown clump under the coffee table.

Quickly, Sam snatched a tissue from the box and cleaned up the mess. For a little dog, Molly sure went a lot.

"Sam, is that you?" His mother called from the bedroom.

"Yup. I'll be there in a sec." He threw the soggy papers in the garbage in the mud room. Then, with Molly nestled in his arms, he went into the bedroom. "Hi," he said.

"How was school this morning?"

"Great," he replied, sitting on the side of her bed.

"Do you have any big projects or tests coming up?"

He thought about the math mid-term on Friday and the English essay he had to hand in on Thursday. He'd have to tell a good sob story to the teacher to get out of that one. "No," he said, shaking his head. "Nothing."

Her eyes showed relief. "That's good. If you had anything big to do, I would insist that you not come home, you know. You can't jeopardize your school work just because I have a broken leg, especially since you're in a new school. Is the work getting a little easier for you?"

"What do you want for lunch?" he asked, hoping the change of topic wasn't too obvious.

She shrugged. "Don't make too much." Then she grinned. "How about a peanut butter sandwich?"

"Peanut butter? I can make Kraft Dinner. Or soup?"

She wagged her finger at him. "Stop spoiling me. Make whatever is easiest and quickest. You only have so much time."

Breakfast dishes littered the kitchen counter. Garbage overflowed under the sink. *Jeepers*, Sam thought. *Why didn't Brian clean up before he left for school like he's supposed to.* Sam pulled the garbage out, tied the top of the bag, and plunked it by the kitchen door. Then he put in a new bag. The dishes would have to wait. Brian could do them when he got home.

Sam put on the water and pasta to make Kraft Dinner. As he stirred, Molly ran around the kitchen in circles, sniffing. Sam knew what that meant. He picked her up and ran to the back door. When he couldn't find any shoes to wear, he went outside in just his socks. Rain fell from a sky the colour of a tin can. Sam wrapped his arms around his body to stop shivering. Molly just sat on the ground and stared up at him.

"Go," he said.

She barked. A bird flew overhead. Suddenly, she took off, chasing the bird.

"No! Molly, come!" Sam ran after her. She bounded around in the rain.

"Come," he said again. She kept running and jumping to get away from him. "I don't want to play," he said.

Molly barked happily. He reached out to pick her up and she darted away from him. Sam chased her, but she thought it was a game. Sam's socks were getting wet and dirty. Finally, he cornered her, diving on the ground, grabbing her in his arms. Now, his pants and shirt were also soaked. He'd have to change for school.

When he got back in the house, the Kraft Dinner was boiling over. He ran down the hall in his wet socks, leaving footprints. He yanked the pan from the stove burner and groaned. There was no water left in the pot. He tried to drain it anyway. An inch of pasta was stuck on the bottom of the pot. He threw the pot in the sink. Crud from the overflowing pasta water had formed under the burner.

Peanut butter sandwiches would have to do. Sam slapped some peanut butter and jam between bread, cut the sandwiches in quarters, and put them on plates.

"I decided to make peanut butter sandwiches," he said to his mom when he entered her room. He gave her one of the plates.

"Perfect." She paused before eating. "What's that smell?" she asked, curling her nose.

"I don't smell anything."

"Did you use the stove?"

"No. I decided to make sandwiches."

Sam wolfed down his sandwich in four bites. Then he wiped his mouth with his hand. "I'd better get back to school," he said.

He thought about the dirty pot in the sink. He didn't have time to clean it. He thought about the garbage bag sitting on the kitchen floor. He didn't have time to take it to the garage.

At the door to his mother's room, he turned to her and said, "Remember what the doctors told you. Stay off your leg. You're only allowed to go to the bathroom."

There was no way Sam wanted his mother to see the disaster in the kitchen.

8 Making a Mess

"You made a mess of that pot," said Brian when Sam got home after school. "You'd better clean it up."

"I will."

"And you left dirty socks on the kitchen floor and footprints all through the house. And your dog destroyed the garbage. You should have seen the mess. She tore up the entire bag and had it everywhere. I wouldn't be surprised if she gets sick. You're supposed to put her in her kennel before you leave the house."

"You have to drive me to practice tonight," said Sam.

"I know. Tell me when you want to go and I'll take you."

"What's for dinner?"

"I think we should order pizza. I don't have time to cook anything. I have to study."

"All you do is study." Sam picked up his backpack.

"Speaking of studying, I left some really important

notes on the end table beside the sofa. Did you see them?"

Sam thought about the papers Molly had chewed earlier. Were they Brian's notes? Sam tried to keep his face neutral as he said, "I didn't see any papers. You probably put them somewhere and you can't find them. You always do stuff like that."

"Yeah, I must have. But where?" Shaking his head, Brian left the kitchen.

Sam listened until he was sure Brian was upstairs then he rushed to the garbage in the mud room. The papers sat on top. He grabbed the papers, ran to the kitchen, and hid them in the garbage under the sink beneath a stinky banana peel and some mouldy cheese.

Although he was supposed to do homework, Sam decided he would rest on his bed for a few minutes. His eyelids felt like five-kilogram bags of salt.

He jumped when Brian barged into his room. "You sleeping?"

"No."

"Whatever. What time is your practice?"

When Sam glanced at his clock, his heart started beating like a ticking time bomb. "We have to go!"

Brain drove so slowly that Sam got antsy. He leaned over to stare at the speedometer. "Can't you drive any faster?"

"I don't want a ticket. Dad will make me pay, and I don't have a lot of cash. It's not my fault you're late."

Brian pressed the button to change the station from rock to country.

Brian knew Sam hated country music. Sam pressed the button to get back to the rock station. Brian turned it back to country.

"I'm driving," said Brian, "so I get to choose the station."

Finally, Brian pulled up to the arena doors. Sam raced into the arena, pulling his heavy bag behind him. Everyone was dressed when he barged into the dressing room. No one said a word to him. It was not cool to be late.

"Sorry," he mumbled.

There was no reply. Not even from Steven.

Sam dressed in record time, but was still a few minutes late getting on the ice. He liked to be the first player on the ice.

Practice went horribly. Sam's arms felt like legs, and his legs like arms. At water break, Steven skated over to Sam. "Try to focus," he whispered.

Sam snapped his helmet in place, ignoring Steven's comment. No one had to tell Sam he wasn't focused. He knew that himself.

"Tomorrow's game is an important one," said Coach Darren in the dressing room after practice. "I want everyone here at least an hour and a half before game time. We need to mentally prepare."

Everyone nodded.

"Eat well, lots of protein." He paused. "Sam, before you take off I want to see you for a few minutes."

All the guys eyed Sam and he felt his throat clog. He nodded, then lowered his head to untie his skates, hoping everyone would stop staring at him.

One by one, everyone except Steven dressed and headed out the door.

"Don't worry," said Steven, once they were alone in the dressing room. "Coach Darren probably wants to make sure your mom's okay."

"Yeah, probably," muttered Sam. His stomach twirled like a broken toy.

"Tell him you'll get lots of rest and be up for tomorrow."

"Yeah, I will."

Steven stood and grabbed his coat off the hook. "Phone me when you get home, okay?"

"Yeah, okay." Sam sucked in a deep breath and neatly placed his pads in his bag.

As soon as Steven left, Coach Darren entered. "Sam, I heard about your mom." He sat down beside Sam on the bench. "How's she feeling?"

"Better." Sam played with the handle of his stick.

"You've had a couple of rough practices." Coach Darren looked Sam directly in the eyes. Sweat beaded on Sam's forehead and he couldn't hold the eye contact. Instead he looked at his stick. "I know," he said. "But I'll be ready for tomorrow."

"Sam, it's okay to be upset about something like this. I can start Jerry tomorrow and let you rest. He's had a few good practices."

"No!" Now it was Sam's turn to stare at Coach Darren. "I'll be fine," he said. "I'll be focused."

* * *

"What took you so long?" Brian was waiting in the empty lobby. "All your teammates left ages ago."

"I had to talk to my coach."

"About what?"

"None of your business."

"Okay. Just asking. Let's blow this joint. I've still got homework to do. And you have clean-up to do."

"Why do I have to clean up?" Sam lugged his heavy bag behind him. It felt as if it was filled with bricks instead of pads.

"I cooked, so you have to clean, little brother."

"You didn't cook. You ordered pizza!"

"Yeah, but I organized it all. Those are the rules. Dad said so."

They drove home in silence. Even the radio wasn't on. Sam slouched in the front seat, his face set in a scowl. Brian never thought of anything but his stupid schoolwork. And he was so messy. Dad called him an absent-minded professor. All he cared about was getting into the best university. Sam wanted a hockey scholarship or a chance to make the NHL, but the way he was playing, none of that would come true for him.

When Sam entered the house he cringed. What a disaster. He gathered up a pile of shoes and coats, stuffed them in the closet, then leaned on the door to get it to close. Finally, he heard it catch. Sam wanted Brian to be the one to open it.

In the kitchen, empty pizza boxes sat on the counters, along with glasses and plates and silverware. Little pieces of trash from Molly's garbage raid littered the floor under the kitchen table. Brain had done a crappy job of sweeping.

"You'd better get busy," said Brian, "or you'll be up until midnight. Andy will freak if he comes home and sees this."

"Can't you help me? I just cleaned up the shoes and coats. And they weren't all mine, you know." He so hoped Brian would go into the closet.

Brian didn't bite. Instead, he crossed his arms over his chest. "It'll cost you. You're supposed to be on kitchen duty. If you want help, you'll have to pay."

Sam gritted his teeth. "How much?"

"My laundry."

Sam thought about his options. With laundry, you just stuffed it in the washing machine. If he got help cleaning the kitchen, he could get to bed earlier. Sam stuck out his hand. "Deal."

They worked quickly. Sam shoved dishes in the dishwasher and Brian wiped the counters. No one swept the floor. Brian figured it would be okay for another day, and Sam agreed.

In the laundry room, Sam glanced at the pile of jeans, T-shirts, and towels on the floor. He picked them all up and tossed them in the washing machine. Once that was done, he let Molly out for a minute. It was so cold outside that she peed and ran back to the door. Sam picked her up and went inside. Then he went in to see his mother.

"How was practice?" she asked, smiling at him.

"Great!" His answer came out really fast and energetic.

"That's good." She pushed his hair off his face. "How's school?"

"Great!" Again his answer spewed from his mouth. Sam thought about the math homework he'd forgotten to do, and the essay he needed to get done. He'd have to milk the teachers for more time.

"You boys are sure doing a super job of running the house." She smiled broadly. "I'm proud of you."

The pile of clothes in Sam's room seemed to be getting bigger every day. He kicked everything under his bed. He'd do *his* laundry tomorrow. And in the morning he'd take his plates and glasses to the kitchen because the dishwasher was already running. Tomorrow. Everything would have to get done tomorrow.

Mom couldn't come out of her bedroom until Friday, so there was lots of time to get things in shape.

Sam flopped down on the bed. Molly whined. He sat up and looked at her. "What's the matter?"

She continued whining. Suddenly, Sam remembered that he had forgotten to feed her. His shoulders sagged. The clock radio on his night table read 11:30 p.m. How did it get to be so late? Practice had ended at 9:45.

Molly continued whining. "Okay," he said. "I'll feed you."

The door to Brian's bedroom was shut, but Sam noticed the light was on. They guy was probably still studying. Sam tiptoed by his room. Downstairs, Sam saw that the light in his mother's room was off. He snuck by her room too. Molly's dish was in the corner of the laundry room.

The washer had finished its cycle. While Sam was waiting for Molly to finish eating, he figured he might as well put the clothes in the dryer.

He started yanking everything out: jeans, a pink T-shirt, another pink T-shirt, pink underwear ... and a big red towel. Oh, no. Sam peered in the washing machine. Everything was pink but the jeans. His eyes bulged when he saw Andy's new Nike shirt. It had gone from pristine white to pale pink.

Sam heard the garage door opening. Andy was home! In a flash, Sam emptied the washing machine, shoving everything in the dryer except the Nike shirt. He looked around the room, saw his backpack, and thrust the wet shirt in with his books.

"Hey," said Andy as he entered the mud room. "What are you still doing up?"

"Um. I had homework to do, and practice, and then I remembered that I forgot to feed Molly so…" He tried to act cool.

"You shouldn't stay up so late, bud. You have school in the morning."

Andy took off his coat and headed to the closet.

"Um, I wouldn't go in there." Sam grimaced.

"Why?" Andy opened the closet door, and coats and shoes spilled out.

"That's why."

"I bet Brian did this," said Andy, kicking at the shoes. "He's such a slob."

Sam nodded. "Yup, it was Brian all right. You should talk to him. Well, I'm off to bed." Sam picked up his backpack and flung it over his shoulder.

"Me too," said Andy. "I have an early meeting, then I have a date tomorrow night at the gym. I want you guys to clean up tomorrow night while I'm out."

Sam frowned. Andy was acting like a father, not a cool big brother. "A date at the gym? That's a weird place for a date."

"No, it's not, little brother." Andy puffed out his chest and winked at Sam. "You think I spend half my paycheque on gym clothes for nothing? She's blonde and she's hot. And fit to boot."

"Come on, Molly," said Sam, faking a smile. "Time for bed." He cringed inside, knowing the gym shirt Andy wanted to wear was now pink.

"You know if you feed your dog this late, she'll probably wake you up in the middle of the night to go out," said Andy.

Sam ignored Andy's comment. "Are you sure you can go on a date? Dad will be mad if you mess things up at work."

Andy grinned and tousled Sam's hair. "I can handle it. Don't worry about me. Worry about working with Brian to keep the house in order. And getting to bed earlier. Every goalie needs rest. I'll do my job for dad and you do yours, and everything will be cool. One day you'll understand, little brother."

Oh, Sam understood all right. Andy wanted to wear his new shirt to impress a girl and Sam had ruined it.

9 Brian's Secret

Molly started whining and scratching on her kennel door at three in the morning.

"Go to sleep." Sam pulled his pillow over his head.

But she wouldn't quit.

"What is wrong with you?" He opened up the kennel door. She immediately put her nose to the carpet and ran in her usual circles.

Sam moaned, picked her up, and headed to the front door. The wind howled in his ears and the wind blew through his pyjamas as he stood on the front porch watching his puppy search for the perfect spot. His eyes felt as if they had gravel stuck under the lids, and he knew if he closed them he could fall asleep standing up. Did Mom do this? Get up in the night with Molly?

Probably. She did everything to keep the family running.

"Hurry up," said Sam to Molly. Why did she have to take so long?

★ ★ ★

"Where's my new white Nike shirt?" Andy stomped from the laundry room to the kitchen. Sam kept his head down and shovelled cereal into his mouth. Milk dribbled from his chin.

"I put it in the laundry room," said Andy.

"Sam did the laundry last night," replied Brian, eyeing Sam.

"I didn't see it." Sam refused to look at either brother.

"How could it disappear?" Andy sounded peeved.

"Maybe it stunk so much from your sweat that it got up and walked away." Brian chortled at his own joke. Sam laughed, but only to get his brother's angry eyes off him. He hoped Andy would get mad at Brian for making jokes. Andy glared at both of them and clomped out of the room.

Sam left for school early to avoid Brian ordering him around. Dazed from lack of sleep, he slowly placed one foot in front of the other. Was this what sleep walking felt like?

Steven met him at the front doors of the school. "Hey," he said. "You didn't call me last night. How did the meeting with Coach Darren go?"

Sam shrugged. "It was good."

"Really?" Steven furrowed his eyebrows.

Sam avoided looking at Steven. Steven was the last

person he wanted to know why Coach Darren talked to him.

"He just wanted to prep me for the game," said Sam. "No big deal."

"Oh, that's cool then. I thought he might, you know…"

"Might what?"

"Nothing," said Steven quietly.

"Are you all right? You look like you just woke up."

"I'm okay," said Sam.

At his locker, Sam unzipped his backpack and groaned. The wet shirt had soaked through his textbooks and notebooks, leaving them with a pink tinge. Gross.

Steven burst out laughing when Sam pulled out his waterlogged textbook. "What happened?"

Sam pulled out a sopping notebook. "That is nasty," said Erica. She had her hand over her mouth to hide her giggles. "That's not good, Sam. I wouldn't show Mr. Snarl-face. He hates it when students wreck books. You'll get a huge lecture that will go on forever. He'll make you pay for the text." She wrinkled her nose. "Do you have your homework in that notebook?"

"Yeah," replied, Sam even though he hadn't done his homework, hadn't even opened his notebook the night before.

"I'd be afraid to go to class," said Erica. "You know how sometimes he surprises us by counting homework as marks, like they were quizzes."

"I'll tell him my mom is sick." Sam nodded his head.

"That *might* work," replied Erica. The creases in her forehead showed her doubt.

★ ★ ★

The school day started horribly and ended horribly. Math was first period and Snarl-face did indeed lecture Sam. He gave him zero on his homework until he could bring in a note from home. And English was last period. Sam tried to sweet-talk his English teacher, tell her how sick his mom was, but when he asked for an extension on his essay, she repeated that he'd need a note from home. It was school policy.

Sam couldn't ask his mom to write him a note. She'd wonder why he wasn't doing his homework.

All the way home, he thought about how he could solve the homework issue. His best plan was to get Andy to write a note for him, seeing as he was sort of acting like Dad right now. If Sam wrote the note, Andy might sign it without looking at it, if Sam told him it was about a field trip or something like that. But Andy was working weird hours, and he had his *date* tonight. Sam would have to either wait up or nab Andy first thing in the morning. And he'd have to make sure Brian the Brain, Mr. Perfect at school, didn't find out or he'd squeal to Mom.

★ ★ ★

For dinner, Brian made some gross concoction that had vegetables and hot dogs in it, and he put it over half-cooked pasta. Mom sometimes made a similar meal, but she used nice fat sausages and fresh vegetables (no horrible frozen peas), and she cooked her pasta until it was soft. Why did Brian cook the hot dogs until they were as rubbery as used car tires? Sam almost barfed when he took his first mouthful. When Brian wasn't looking, he dumped the whole mess in the garbage and made himself a peanut butter sandwich.

Although it tasted awful, Mom went on and on about how good it was.

"You really like it?" asked Sam, scrunching up his face. "I thought it was terrible."

"Brian just needed to cook the pasta a bit longer." She smiled when she chewed. "It's not that bad." She swallowed with huge effort.

"You're just trying to be nice." Sam reached for her water glass. "Here," he said, "wash it down."

"Sam," she shook her head at him. "Brian tried his best." She paused. "Your dad phoned today."

"How's he doing?"

"Wonderful. He's excited about this project. He wanted to know how you and Brian were getting along. And he really wishes he could be here for your game tonight."

Sam nodded.

"So, how are you boys getting along?"

"Good." After last night, with Brian driving like a turtle, Sam had asked Steven for a ride to hockey.

"I was thinking of venturing out into the kitchen tonight. I'm going to ask Brian to help me. If I lean on him, it shouldn't put too much weight on my leg."

Sam thought about the chaos of pots and pans that Brian had created when he cooked the dinner. The guy had used every dish and left them all in the sink. And Sam was on kitchen duty. Just because he was youngest, Sam had to always do the clean-up, and tonight he didn't have time until after his game.

"I don't think that's a good idea, Mom," he said. "You can't put *any* pressure on your leg."

"Well, we'll see. I'll talk to Brian."

When Sam left his mom's room, he raced upstairs. He barged into Brian's room without knocking. "You can't help Mom out of her room tonight."

Brian looked up from his books, annoyance written all over his face. The top of his forehead was creased like an old wrinkly apple. "Could you knock?" he barked.

"I don't have time to clean up your stinking mess. So don't let Mom come out of her room."

Brian held up his hand. "What do you mean let Mom out of her room?"

"Mom wants you to help her walk to the kitchen tonight."

"You'd better get busy on those dishes."

"I don't have time. The Beckers are picking me up soon. I still have to organize my equipment."

"Remember what Dad said. We have to work together. Tonight I cooked a super-duper meal and now it's your turn to clean up."

"Yeah, well, that was before you used every pot in the kitchen to make such a crappy dinner, and I had to organize a ride for myself because you're such a bad driver."

"I'd like to see you to do better."

"Tomorrow night, I'm cooking." Sam pointed to his chest.

"Whatever," retorted Brian. "Nice job on the laundry, by the way."

"Be quiet."

"Did you wreck Andy's new shirt? The one he wanted to wear for his hot date?"

"So, will you promise not to let Mom come out of her room tonight?"

Brian leaned back in his chair and looked at Sam. Sam felt his blood boiling and his heart thumping.

The guy was being a jerk. "Can't you for once do something nice for me?" Sam could feel tears behind his eyes. This always happened. Brian was a nasty brother.

Brian slammed his chair down. "You have no idea how nice I've been to you." He turned to stare at Sam as if he had some amazing secret.

"Yeah, right."

"Do you know that I've got a friend at school who's going to your game tonight? I was going to go with him but Mom needs me at home."

"I didn't know you had any friends." Sam was still peeved at him, but his curiosity was piqued.

"This friend plays for the Ottawa 67's. I invited him to watch you."

"Get out of here! You don't know anyone from that team."

"Yeah, I do. I tutor him because he has to miss so much school. He's actually really smart, and if he doesn't get into the NHL, he wants to be a dentist."

"What's his name?"

"Justin Landry."

"He's the 67's number-one goalie!" Sam's eyes widened. Could Brian be telling the truth? Sam had been to a 67's game. Landry was amazing. He played exactly how Sam wanted to play. His reflexes were so fast and he was aggressive, always coming out of the net. And he was the only goalie in the OHL who could fire the puck up the ice and have it land right on a player's stick, like a pass. In the game Sam had seen, Landry had got an assist.

Brian looked amused. "You're awful quiet. Listen, I told him you were good. He and another one of the 67's, who knows the brother of your friend Steven Becker, are going tonight."

"I don't believe you."

"Suit yourself. Oh, by the way, not only do I get the best junior goalie to come watch you play but … I've been taking care of your dog. I let her out three times today." He casually leaned back in his chair and put his hands behind his head. "You know, little brother, you need to learn how to prioritize. You're running in circles."

"I am not," Sam retorted, knowing that Brian had hit a nerve.

Brian grinned like Jim Carrey as the Grinch. "Since I'm such a *super* nice guy, I'll let *your* dog out while you're playing hockey for a million hours tonight, and keep Mom out of the kitchen for you. But you have to make breakfast and clean up all the dishes by tomorrow morning. This is called working together, you know. Teamwork. Just because you're a goalie doesn't mean you're the only one on the team."

Sam tilted his head. Was this for real?

Brian held up his hand. "I'll play some cards with Mom and keep her away from your mess."

Sam nodded. "Thanks," he mumbled.

"You're welcome." Brian smiled. "Good luck tonight. I'd come watch if I didn't have to take care of Mom."

Sam walked to the door. Brian wasn't actually that bad a brother.

He had his hand on the door when Brian said, "By the way. I take my eggs over-easy with a little pepper and lots of salt. Oh, and I want whole wheat toast and fried tomatoes, and either bacon or sausage."

"Eggs?!" Sam turned and glared at Brian.

Brian's face was one huge grin. "Just kidding."

10 Too Many Goals

Sam decided to avoid the kitchen before he left so he wouldn't have to see the mess. Unfortunately, the mess had become like a big blob, spreading its way from the kitchen into all the other rooms in the house. Jackets, shoes, newspapers — even plates with crusts of bread — seemed to be in places they shouldn't be. Sam had to ignore the mess, since he didn't have the time to do anything about it.

When Sam heard the horn honking outside, he said goodbye to his mother.

"Good luck, honey," she said from her bed. She gave him the thumbs-up. "I know you'll be fabulous in net tonight, as always."

"Thanks."

"I'll wait up for you. You have to promise to tell me every last play."

Sam bobbed his head. "You bet."

In the back of the Becker's van, Sam hoisted his

big bag up and placed it beside Steven's. Steven sat in the front passenger seat, so Sam hopped in the side door.

Steven turned around. "Guess who is coming to our game tonight!"

"Who?"

"Carl Guthrie and Justin Landry of the Ottawa 67's! I'm so excited. They're friends of my brother."

"Wow," said Sam, "that's cool." He still couldn't believe that Brian knew a hockey player from the 67's.

Sam entered the dressing room pumped to play, or so he thought. He sat down on the bench and leaned against the wall for a minute to breathe. He'd hardly stopped all day. School, home, school, chores — Sam was exhausted. With all that he had to do before he got here, he didn't get to do his pre-game ritual.

When was Mom going to be better?

When was Dad coming home?

He thought about the dirty dishes, the papers lying haphazardly in every room, the sticky floor, and the lint on the carpet, and he sighed. Dad had better not come home any time soon. Sam had to make dinner tomorrow. What would he make? Kraft Dinner was the only thing he knew.

"Hey, Sam, wake up," whispered Steven. "You have to look alive. You're in net tonight. This is a big game."

Sam shook his head and unzipped his bag, pulling out his gear. How could he be thinking of what to make for dinner when he had such an important game to play?

Without thinking, Sam got dressed. When he reached behind to cinch the straps on his pads, he suddenly realized he'd tied up his right skate before his left.

Once dressed, Sam sat back, waiting for Coach Darren to come in and give his pre-game speech. Sam's stomach grumbled and he hoped the peanut-butter sandwich would carry him through the game. He closed his eyes, willing himself to focus instead of sleep. Every time he tried to think of making a save, he also thought of crawling into bed after the game was over. He'd never felt this tired before a game.

Coach Darren worked hard in the dressing room to fire up the team. At first he spoke quietly, telling them what they had to do, running through the plays. Then his voice got louder, his face got more animated, and his hands motioned decisively. Just after Coach Ernie announced that the ice was ready, they got in a huddle for their team cheer. The noise echoed off the dressing-room walls, giving Sam his adrenalin shivers. He breathed deep to focus his energy inward.

Sam stepped on the ice and skated a few laps to loosen up. Then he stretched out with Jerry in the corner while the rest of the team continued skating. Sam sunk into splits and leaned his body forward to stretch out his lower back, hip flexor, and hamstring muscles. Jerry did the same stretches.

Once he was in his net, Sam skated back and forth in his crease, trying to rough up the ice. He heard Steven call for the team to begin their warm-up drills. Sam faced forward, ready to catch the shots.

The first few players came down and fired their first shots in holes. Sam missed every shot. Then it was Steven's turn. He did the same thing!

"Give me a chance to warm up," he yelled through his mask.

"I didn't shoot it hard," said Steven.

"Whatever," mumbled Sam.

He managed a few good saves before Coach Darren called them over to the bench for the team cheer.

Then the whistle blew.

Sam batted both goalposts and got in his ready position. The puck dropped at centre ice and the Kings took possession. They skated toward Cumberland's net. Sam would have preferred being the goalie facing the first shot on net. It made him get into the game right away. The Kings took a shot from the blue line and Cumberland's goalie made an easy glove save. A face-off was called in Cumberland's end.

Again the puck was controlled by the Kings. This time Steven wound up for a shot just outside the hash marks. The goalie batted it away with his blocker. Sam intently watched the action taking place on the other end of the ice. The puck was loose.

It got picked up by a Cumberland player, who

skated a few strides before he made a great pass to get his team out over their own blue line. The Kings' defence skated to get back. In a slick move, a Cumberland forward rushed by one of Sam's defence. Steven had warned Sam that this guy was good, a slick stick-handler and a goal-scorer. Sam accessed his situation. Two Cumberland players were heading toward him on a two-on-one. Steven and Alex were back-checking, but Sam knew they wouldn't catch the two forwards who were barrelling down on him.

He kept his eyes on the puck. His defence played the middle.

The Cumberland player wound up for a slapshot. Sam was ready.

But Cumberland pulled a fake. As soon as Sam realized that, he shuffled across his net. If it was one-timed he could be in trouble. He saw the player wind up to take a shot, and Sam whipped his hand up, but the puck sailed into the top corner of the net. First shot of the night and it had gone in.

Sam was one for one.

Frustrated, he smacked his stick against the side of his net. He hated letting the first shot in.

"Don't worry," said Steven, hitting his stick against Sam's pads. "We'll get it back."

Sam nodded.

For the next ten minutes of play, Sam only had to face three shots and they were easy saves. Most of the play was in the other end, and the Kanata Kings were definitely outplaying the Cumberland Giants. Sam wanted someone to bury the puck to tie the score. Steven came close. As he watched, Sam wished the play was in his end just a little more than it was. He found it difficult to stay warm and focused when there were so few shots.

With two minutes left in the period, there had been maybe five shots on Sam. Finally, however, the face-off was in his end. Sam crouched and held his glove out to the side. The puck dropped, there was a scramble, and a few bodies fell right in front of him. Sam lost sight of the puck. He shuffled back and forth. Where was it?

Suddenly, he saw it in front of him. He decided to go down and pounce on it, but just as he got to his knees, a Cumberland player swiped at it with a backhand shot, lofting it in the air. Sam was already halfway down and didn't have time to get up. The puck cruised over his shoulder. It made his stomach sick to see the puck in the back of the net.

Why had he gone down? It had been years since he'd made that kind of mistake. Sam hung his head.

At the end of the first period he didn't have to look at the scoreboard to know his team was losing 2–0. And both goals scored on him had been weak, goals he should have stopped.

At the start of the second period, Sam skated to

his net with intensity, determined to do better.

The puck bounced when it was dropped and ended up on a Giants' stick. Sam squatted, tightening up his leg muscles to hold his position. Sweat dripped down his face.

The Giants' forward skated to the outside along the boards. He tried to duck under the Kings' defence but was pinned. He pushed the puck down the boards to his centre, who had skated in for support. Sam held his pad firm against the side of the net and his stick on the ice, ready for a bad-angle shot. But the Giants' centre skated behind the back of the net. Sam saw the Giants' winger open in front of him. Where were the Kings? Why weren't they on this man?

"Cover the man out front," he yelled.

Sam positioned his body in front to stop the possible shot. Suddenly, he realized the centre behind the net wasn't going to pass the puck, he was going to go for a wrap-around. Sam slid across his net.

The Giants' centre pushed the puck by Sam's stick and by his pads. Sam thought he had it. The ref blew his whistle and made the motion.

Goal.

Sam moaned. He'd let a goal in on a wrap-around. He hadn't done that since Tyke hockey.

Sam guzzled some water and snapped his cage down. He glanced up at the score board: 3–0 for the Cumberland Giants.

He bent over and shook his head. He had to focus.

The play went up and down the ice. Sam made his saves no problem. He was back on track.

The ref called a face-off in the Kings' end. When the puck dropped, the two centres battled it out. Then the puck went back to the Giants' defence. There were too many men in Sam's crease. He couldn't see.

"You're screening me!" He tried to push players out of his way.

The defence wound up for a slapshot. The puck hit Sam's pads and bounced out. It landed in front. Sam pounced on it, covering it with his glove. A Giants' player aggressively poked under Sam's glove, jabbing at the puck.

When was the ref going to blow the whistle?

The player kept jabbing. Sam looked for someone to lob the puck to. Steven cross-checked the Giants' player, knocking him forward. The guy jabbed Sam as he was going down. The whistle blew. The Giants' players started jumping up and down. Sam looked behind him.

The puck was in the net.

No way!

Sam came out of his net and skated toward the ref. "That wasn't a goal," he yelled.

"The puck was in before the whistle blew," replied the ref.

"No, it wasn't!"

"Sam, take it easy." Steven put his arm around Sam skated him back to his net. "Let it go. We'll get the next one in."

Sam heard his name from the bench. When he looked over he saw the open gate and Jerry stepping onto the ice, his mask on and his stick in his hand.

Sam was getting pulled.

11 Taking the Blame

Coach Darren motioned for Sam to come to the bench. Sam had never been pulled in the middle of a game for not playing well.

Jerry swished by him with long strides, heading toward the net. Sam's stomach lurched and the skin on his face felt hot and clammy. Stepping onto the bench, he avoided looking at the guys. He heard Steven trying to talk to him, but Sam refused to acknowledge the voice.

Coach Darren stepped down from his standing perch and walked to the end of the bench. He put his hand on Sam's shoulder.

"Will I get to go back in?" Sam asked without making eye contact with Coach Darren.

"We'll see."

Sam felt the tears stinging behind his eyes. He couldn't cry. It wouldn't help. Even when Coach Darren had moved away from Sam and back to the middle of the bench, Sam decided to leave his helmet on.

By the end of the second period, Sam had to admit that Jerry had made some unbelievable saves. He had pulled a Marty Brodeur butterfly save, and he had and stopped a wrist shot that everyone thought was in for sure.

As the Zamboni came on the ice for a between-periods flood, Sam made sure he was the last person off the bench. Once in the dressing room, Sam thought Coach Darren might tell him that he could go back in for the third period, but he didn't.

No one said anything to Sam. Sam's face burned with a horrible heat. The fact that the Kings were losing 4–0 was his fault.

His stomach heaved up and down as if he was seasick. He was so disappointed in himself. How could he have let in all those goals? They weren't even good goals.

When the ice was ready, the Kings filed out to the bench. Sam made his way to his spot at the end. He didn't want to sit, so he stood with his chin on top of his stick to watch.

The Cumberland Giants fired shot after shot at Jerry, and he made the saves. The intensity of the game seemed to pick up and the crowd started going wild, chanting Jerry's name. The guy was definitely standing on his head.

Then the Kings had a breakaway. Steven raced toward the net. Sam held his breath. Steven deked and fired. His shot hit the top corner and dropped. He jumped in the air and was smothered by the rest of the guys on the ice. The Kings on the bench went crazy too.

Sam glanced up at the scoreboard to see that there was fifteen minutes left to play in the third period. There was still time. It was possible for the Kings to make a comeback.

Right after the face-off, Alex skated down the wing and fired the puck in a quick snap shot from just inside the blue line. Did the Giants' goalie have it in his glove? Sam leaned forward, trying to see the play. The goalie must have fumbled it, because Sam saw the puck land out front. Steven was instantly at the net and nailed it.

Again, the Kings' bench went crazy. Sam smacked his hands on the boards. He wished he was on the ice.

The Giants played gritty defensive hockey and held the Kings off, even though they kept peppering the Giants' goalie with shots. But with three minutes left, he couldn't hang on any longer and the Kings scored again!

Now the score was 4–3 for the Giants.

Coach Darren pulled the guys in for a time-out. "One goal, guys. That's all we need. Drive to the net. You have to play aggressive offensive hockey to tie it up."

A bad bounce for the Kings put the puck on the stick of the best Giants forward. He sped past the Kings defence, creating a breakaway. Sam stared at Jerry. He was too far back in his net. He needed to come out a bit, challenge the shooter.

Sam sucked in a deep breath as he watched the Giants forward wind up for the shot. The puck was heading toward the open side of Jerry's net. Jerry stacked his pads and slid. The puck deflected out. He'd made the save!

"Great save, Jerry!" The guys on the bench went crazy.

With one minute left, Coach Darren pulled Jerry to give the Kings the extra attacker.

"Good job," said Sam, as Jerry took his place beside him.

"Thanks." Jerry's grin went from ear to ear.

The Kings played aggressively, hitting two posts. They kept pounding the puck at the Giants' goalie, but he kept making saves.

Time ran out. The final score was 4–3.

Sam wanted to throw up. If he had of played well right from the beginning, the Kings would have won.

Sam undressed, keeping his head down. He didn't say a word to anyone, and no one said anything to him. Coach Darren met him outside the door. "Sam, can I talk to you?" he said.

"Yeah."

The coach put his hand on Sam's shoulder. "I know things are a bit stressful for you at home right now."

Sam lowered his head.

"I'm going to play Jerry for the next few games because we're playing some weaker teams. It will be good for him."

"But you told me I'm the number-one goalie," said Sam softly.

"I'm just giving you a little break," said Coach Darren, patting him on the back. Just then Steven came out of the dressing room.

Sam plodded down the hall, his feet feeling like heavy weights. Steven walked beside him. "What did Coach want?"

"Nothing," said Sam. "The loss is my fault. I should be able to handle this."

"We're a team."

"I let the goals in. Our loss was my fault."

Steven furrowed his eyebrows. "Why do goalies always take the blame?"

"I only take the blame when it's my fault. This loss was all because of me. If you make a mistake, it's not the same as when I do. When I make a mistake, the goal goes up on the board."

Out in the lobby, Sam saw two guys talking to Mr. Becker and Steven's older brother. Sam groaned. Why had Justin Landry and Carl Guthrie picked this game to watch? The night his parents weren't here. Sam wanted to go home.

"Let's go talk to my dad," said Steven, his eyes lighting up. "He's talking to Justin Landry and Carl Guthrie. I want to meet them."

"I think I'll get a drink first." Sam hoped that, by the time he waited in line at the concession, the guys would be gone.

But his plan didn't work. The line was short and the service fast, so they were all still talking when Sam had his drink. He had to go over to them; Mr. Becker was his ride home. He slowly approached the group.

"Hi, Sam," said Mr. Becker.

"Hi," Sam mumbled with his head down.

No one was going to say "good game" to him. Not tonight.

"That was a tough loss," said Justin Landry.

Sam glanced up for a second. Justin was eyeing him. Sam quickly put his head down and stared at the toe of his shoe. "Yeah," he muttered.

"We have good days and bad days. You have to deal with them all." Justin patted Sam on the back.

Sam nodded his head but he wasn't sure if he agreed with him. He stood silent as the 67's players complimented Steven on his play. When they presented Steve and Sam with passes to watch a 67's practice, Sam mumbled his thanks and stuffed the card in his pocket. He sure didn't deserve a treat like that, not after the way he played.

"You guys will beat Cumberland next time you play them," said Mr. Becker on the ride home.

Sam slumped in the back seat and stared out the window.

"Don't worry, Sam," said Mr. Becker, trying to catch Sam's eyes in the rear view mirror. "Even the pros have bad games."

"Yeah," piped up Steven. "Even the pros. You'll be back on track next game."

Sam gazed out the window. What Steven didn't know was that Jerry was going to play net for the next few games.

So the next game for Sam might not be for a while.

12 Working as a Team

The house was quiet when Sam entered. Molly ran toward him, wagging her tail. He picked her up and nuzzled his cheek against her nose. Her breath had that puppy smell. She started licking his face and it made him feel a bit better.

None of the guys except Steven had talked to Sam after the game. All the congratulations had gone to Jerry for helping the team come back, for playing such a stellar game. Sam could tell that the team thought he had played lousy, and that he was the reason why they had lost.

A light shone under his mother's door. If she wasn't laid up in bed, he'd cry and tell her everything. But he couldn't make her feel worse than she already did. He'd have to put on a brave face for her.

Before he ventured into his mother's room, he peeked in the kitchen. Someone had done some clean-up. Only a few dishes were stacked in the sink.

Sam slowly pushed open the door to his mom's room. She was sitting up, reading. When she heard the noise, she looked at him over the rim of her reading glasses, put a bookmark in her book, and snapped it shut.

"So … how was the game?" she asked, smiling at him.

"We lost." Sam walked toward her.

"That's too bad. Was it a close game?"

"4–3."

"Tell me about it."

"We almost scored in the end, but we just couldn't put it in the net."

"Wish I could have been there. It sounds like an exciting game to watch." She patted the bed.

Sam nodded and sat on the edge of the bed. "I guess they've never lost to this team."

"Were you happy with how you played?"

Sam smiled a big fake smile. "Yeah," he replied. "It was a close game, but I played okay. All the goals were good goals, breakaways and two-on-ones. They've got one really good forward." He couldn't believe he was lying so well.

She reached for his hand and squeezed it. "There are lots of games left in the season."

He nodded, unable to speak.

"Somehow," she pointed her finger at him and continued, "I'm getting to the rink to watch your next game. I'm getting very tired of sitting around." She winked. "Maybe I can get a wheelchair to get me there."

This time when Sam nodded, his stomach was spinning in circles. There was no way she could come to his next game. She couldn't. She just couldn't.

He was sitting on the bench.

When Sam left his mom's room, he told her he was going straight to bed. Instead he tiptoed to the kitchen. He wanted to prove to Andy and Brian that he could handle his responsibilities. Good thing there was only one load of dishes to do because that was all Sam had the energy to do. Sam's eyelids drooped as he quietly unloaded the dishwasher and put the dirty dishes from the sink into the dishwasher.

The dishwasher was completely full when Sam finished. He glanced at the clock on the stove. Midnight already. Sam never went to bed at midnight on school nights. He trudged up the stairs, carrying Molly.

"Don't wake me up too early, okay?" He nuzzled her fur.

Entering his bedroom, he saw his backpack and his books. Another night and he'd not done any homework. A low moan came from inside his body. He was in big trouble. And how was he going to get a note from Andy.

Suddenly, Sam had an idea. He yanked his homework out of his bag and gave it to Molly. "Chew this," he whispered. "Andy will have to write me a note if you wreck my homework."

Sam played tug-of-war with Molly, giggling when she ripped all his homework to shreds. This was actually kind of fun.

When his work was completely unreadable, he crawled under his covers.

"Good girl," he said, petting Molly. "For being such a good homework-wrecker you can sleep on my pillow."

Sam slept soundly. Molly woke him up at seven by licking his face.

"Go back to sleep," he said to her.

Then he heard the knock on his bedroom door. "Wake up, little brother," said Brian.

Sam flung his pillow across his room. "Go away."

Brian swung open the door. "Hey, what's all that paper?" Brian asked.

Sam threw his covers on the floor and jumped out of bed.

"Oh, no," moaned Sam. He looked at Molly, who gazed up at him, innocent and cute, wagging her tail, wanting to play. He turned back to Brian. "She ruined my homework!"

"That's a drag. You're teacher won't be too happy."

"I'll have to ask Andy to give me a note." Sam tried to say the words so they didn't sound rehearsed.

"Andy?" Brian scratched his head. "Just get Mom

to write the note. She doesn't write with her leg."

"I don't want to bother her." Sam hurried his reply.

"Whatever. There's only thing wrong with your plan. Andy's not home."

Startled, Sam stared at Brian. "Why isn't Andy home?"

"He left at six-thirty. He had a big meeting this morning."

"You're kidding, right?"

Brian raised his eyebrows at Sam. "Hel-*lo*. What do I possibly have to gain from kidding about Andy going to work early?"

"Well, that's not good," stuttered Sam. "He's supposed to be making Mom breakfast."

"Slammer, it's not a big deal. I don't have a class until ten today. I told him we'd do it."

"Can … you write me a note then?"

Brian tilted his head. "I'll do better. I'll help you with your homework tonight."

"Really? You'll help me?"

"Sure. You can't do it all you know."

"Thanks. Hey, I'll make you breakfast."

Brian held his thumb up. "Now, that's teamwork."

The first egg that Sam cracked into the pan broke. He shoved it to the side and cracked another. This time it spread perfectly, the yolk remaining a big golden ball. He cracked a few more and they all worked too. As the white part of the egg cooked, it started to bubble and pop. Sam carefully flipped them. And he had thought that all he could make was Kraft Dinner.

He stared at the pan. What was he going to do about his homework? Brian said he'd help tonight, but that didn't take care of today.

Suddenly, a flash of light went on his head. He had a great idea!

He finished making breakfast, called Brian to come for breakfast, and made a plate for his mother.

"Sam, you don't have to make me eggs. Toast is good enough." She graciously accepted her food. "I feel so badly that you boys are waiting on me like this."

Sam smiled. "I don't mind."

"You're such a good boy." She glanced at the clock by her bed. "You'd better get going. You'll be late for school." She dunked her toast in the egg yolk. "I can take my plate to the kitchen."

"Brian's home until ten," said Sam. "I'll tell him to get it."

"No," she said. "I have to get up. I can't stand this anymore."

As soon as Sam left his mother's room, he rushed to find Brian. "Mom's talking about walking around again!"

"Are you serious?" Brian immediately turned to look at Sam.

"Ye-*ah!* Sam bobbed his head. "This morning. And I have to go to school."

"Okay, listen," said Brian, glancing around at the messy kitchen. "Let's clean this up real fast. Then we'll fill the closets. That will be good enough. She won't bend over to look under anything. She can't, her cast is too big. Then later we'll fix everything."

Sam nodded. Both boys worked as if they were set on fast-forward. They emptied the dishwasher and refilled it. Whatever dirty dishes were left, they shoved in the oven. That was Sam's idea, and for once Brian thought something he said was clever. Then Sam ran a dishcloth under water, threw it on the ground, and moved it around with his foot to wash the floor.

"Gross," he said when he picked it up. The cloth was black. He tossed it in the washing machine along with a bunch of other clothes that were lying around. He shut the lid of the machine, but Brian said not to turn it on because they shouldn't wash whites with jeans.

They threw shoes in the closet, and stuffed newspapers, magazines, and even some garbage under the sofa. Brian fed Molly the stale, leftover food.

"I hope she doesn't barf," said Sam.

"You'd better get going," replied Brian, ignoring Sam's comment. "The place looks okay."

"Sure," said Sam, putting his backpack on his shoulder.

Stepping outside, Sam started walking toward the school. Partway there, he stopped and flipped open the cell phone he'd received for Christmas. His parents gave it to him for emergencies. Well, today was an emergency.

He had the school absent line written on a little piece of paper he'd shoved in his pocket. He dialed, took a deep breath, and pressed Send.

When the answering machine asked for name, class, and reason for absence, he said in a low voice, "This is Sam Watson's father. He's in 8-2 and has the flu." He exhaled a huge breath and snapped his phone shut. With Brian's help tonight, Sam would be all caught up by tomorrow. No one would ever know he wasn't really sick.

13 Cutting the Angle

Just like a detective or a cop from a television show, Sam slithered along the side of his house. Brian was probably in the kitchen or in his room. But he could be with Mom. If Sam could sneak in the door that led to the walk-out basement without them seeing him, he could stay downstairs for the entire day. He had a lunch in his bag and his Mp3 player. He could sleep, listen to tunes, and read a magazine. He also had Roy McGregor's latest Screech Owl book to read. Sam knew Brian wouldn't be downstairs watching television or playing pool when he had work to do, not Brian the Brain.

Before he'd left, Sam had made sure the walk-out door was unlocked.

Sam felt in his pocket for the treat he'd brought along for Molly, just in case she heard him and came running. As he fingered the treat, he felt something else. It was the card Justin Landry had given him, the pass that could get him into a 67's practice. On the back he'd written their practice schedule for the next week. They had a practice today, a light skate, because they had a game tonight. Sam wished he played for that team so he had an excuse not to go to school.

Sam slid open the door. Once inside, he eased it shut, then tiptoed to the couch. When he saw the blanket and pillow someone had left out, he nestled in, thinking a morning nap would be perfect.

Then he heard the footsteps on the stairs leading to the basement.

He immediately sat up. Who was coming downstairs? Where should he hide?

He scooted behind the reclining chair and hunkered into a squat, his arms circling his knees. And he crossed his fingers.

Brian whistled as he strutted toward the pool table. What was he doing?

Sam peeked around the chair to see Brian pulling the cover off the pool table. He took a pool cube from the stand. This was too weird. Why was Brian playing pool now? Sam continued peering around the chair to watch Brian lining up the balls on the pool table.

"Okay," Brian said to himself. "If I set the ball here and I try to hit the ball on a 43 degree angle…" He took a protractor from his back pocket and lined up the angle of the ball.

Sam put his hand to his mouth to stop himself

from laughing. Brian was doing math on the pool table! As Sam watched Brian, he remembered the goalie summer camp he'd attended and how the instructor had used a pool table to demonstrate cutting down the goal angles. It was funny to see Brian doing the same thing. Maybe he should ask Brian to help him. The very thought made Sam smile.

Sam's legs began to cramp and he desperately wanted to get out of the position he was in. But he didn't dare move.

Finally, Brian nodded his head as if he was satisfied with his answers. He laid the pool cue on top of the table and headed up the stairs, forgetting to put the cover back on the table. Sam shook his head. No wonder the house was a mess.

When Sam was sure Brian was upstairs, he stood and stretched. His legs ached from being in one position for so long. Once he had the kinks out, Sam flopped down on the couch again, curling up under the blanket.

He must have slept. When he woke up, he heard voices upstairs. And a loud thumping sound.

Sam sat up and listened. He heard someone talking to Brian, and it wasn't Mom. It was Dad! And they were in the living room. The loud thumping must be Mom!

Dad wasn't supposed to be back until tomorrow. Why was he home? Sam glanced at his watch. It was just 9:30. Sam had slept for an hour.

He tossed the blanket off and crept to the bottom of the stairs.

"Get your things, Brian, and I'll take you to school today," said Dad.

Sam heard Brian going up to his room. Sam's entire body sagged in relief. They were leaving.

"I won't be gone long," Sam's father said to his mother.

"Don't worry about me," Sam heard Mom say. "I'm just fine. If you have to be at the office, go ahead. I'm going to park myself in the living room with my book and the picture window."

"I'll let the dog out before I go," said Dad. "I hope she doesn't throw up again. When will Sam be home?" Sam's body went rigid when his father mentioned his name.

"I told him to stay for lunch today," replied his mother. "The boy is worn out from running home every day."

"I guess they lost the other night," said his father. "I haven't talked to anyone yet about the game, but I might phone the coach."

Phone the coach! Oh, no! Sam's eyes widened. Dad would find out he got pulled and was not going to play because he couldn't handle the pressure at home. He'd promised his dad he could do it.

"Sam was happy with how he played," said his mother. "That counts for a lot."

Sam cringed. His little white lies were getting out of hand. He squeezed his eyes shut. They couldn't find out that he'd skipped school. Everything would be okay if no one found out anything. Brian would help him with his homework and he'd start playing better hockey. Everything could be normal again.

"When I get back from the office, I'll fix a few things in the basement."

Sam stiffened. What? Why didn't he go to the office for the whole day, like he always did? Since they'd moved to Ottawa, the man worked 24/7. Why did he want to fix things today?

"You don't have to stay home for me," said Mom.

"I need a day at home too," replied Dad.

Right, thought Sam. *And where am I supposed to go?*

As soon as Sam heard the door close and the car leave the garage, he sneaked out of the house. The weather was still damp and rainy. He yanked up his collar and quickly headed out the back gate, shoving his hands in his pockets to keep them warm.

Once on the sidewalk, he pulled out the card his fingers had brushed against in his pocket. The Ottawa 67's were on the ice in an hour. Maybe he could catch a bus out to the Civic Centre and watch the practice. At least he'd have something to do.

★ ★ ★

The bus dropped Sam off across the street from the Civic Centre. Proud for not making any mistakes getting there, and feeling quite free and independent, Sam walked in the direction of the big arena. Since moving to Ottawa, Sam had been to one 67's game. They were a good team and had some good players. Maybe Sam would play for them one day.

He wondered which door he should go in. The main doors would lead to administration offices, and Sam didn't want anyone asking why he wasn't in school.

Sam remembered that at the Calgary Saddledome, there were side entrances to the arena. When Sam was a peewee, his team had a few exhibition games there, and they had always entered through a shipping door at the side of the arena. Maybe it was the same here.

Sam made his way along the side of the big building, looking for a door that could lead to the belly of the arena where the dressing rooms were.

Halfway around, he spotted what looked like a shipping and receiving area. There was a concrete pad for trucks to come in and out, and ... a metal door. He glanced around to see if anyone was watching him. When he was sure he was alone, he ran up the ramp and tried the knob.

It clicked and opened.

14 Handling the Good with the Bad

Sam scooted inside the Civic Centre, closing the heavy door gently behind him. In the distance, he heard skates on ice. The practice had started. A wide hallway with black floor runners loomed in front of him. He didn't see anyone. Everyone was probably watching the practice.

The bellies of these big arenas amazed him. The concrete walls were covered with pictures and photos. There were many doors, leading to offices filled with filing cabinets, and rooms with jerseys, sticks, and equipment. He wanted to be a part of a big team one day.

Suddenly Sam saw a guy with towels draped over his shoulder come out of a room. Sam pressed his back against the wall and held his breath until the trainer passed him, went in a door and disappeared.

Sam breathed. Okay, so now he knew where the trainer's room was. Most of the other team personnel probably had offices down there too. And the dressing rooms would be close by.

At a fast clip, Sam headed away from the offices and kept walking until he saw an alcove that led to the ice. Was this the Zamboni entrance? He ducked into the small hallway. If it was, Sam would be safe here until the practice ended. He had forty minutes to watch.

The hall he stood in was really quiet. Sam edged toward the glass. Once he could see the ice surface, he searched the ice for Justin Landry, whose goalie mask had streaks of blue and red. A magazine article said he had bought a new one when he made the 67's.

Two goalies were on the ice, but neither had a red and blue mask. Maybe Landry had a practice mask. The coach called over the team to explain a drill. Sam couldn't hear what he was saying but, when he saw them line up, he knew exactly what drill they were doing. It was the three-on-two breakout.

The players skated down the ice, weaving over the blue line. Sam stared intently at the goalie in net. He wanted to know how far out in front he held his glove hand, where he kept his blocker hand, what was his stance, and how well he read the play.

When the forward undressed the defence and fired, Sam held his breath. *Wow, what a shot!*

Then he blinked. *What a save!* Sam's eyes widened. That had to be Landry in net. How had he made that save?

Suddenly, Sam felt a hand on his shoulder.

He jumped and turned.

"What are you doing here?" Justin Landry stood beside Sam.

"I'm, uh, watching the practice." Sam's words came out in a big breathless hurry. "How come you're not out there?"

Justin casually put his hands in his jeans pockets. "It was an optional today and I needed a rest. Plus, I had a lot of homework to catch up on. Coach said I could take the morning off. I finished my work so I came down to watch the end of the practice. We have a big game tonight."

"I know," said Sam.

Justin furrowed his eyebrows and tilted his head. "What are you doing here? Don't you have school?"

Sam shuffled on his feet, looking at the ice instead of Justin. "Um, I have spares."

"Spares, eh? I used to do my homework in spares so I wouldn't have to stress at night." He paused. "Where's your school?"

Sam shrugged. "It's not too far from here."

"Did you catch the bus?"

Sam jiggled his leg in nervousness. "Yeah," he said.

"Did it take you long to get here?" Justin had a puzzled look on his face, as if he was calculating a hard math problem.

"Not too long." Sam tried to sound nonchalant.

Justin put his hand on Sam's shoulder. "Listen, bud. When I gave you that practice schedule and invitation, I didn't want you to skip school. That's not good."

Sam's shoulders sagged. He lowered his head. What was he doing? Why was he here? He had lied to the school and lied to his mom, and here he was caught in a web. "I know," he said, shaking his head. He looked up at Justin. "I've never skipped school before."

"Are you still choked about your game the other night?"

"Kind of."

"Let it go," said Justin. "Everyone has bad games."

"I'd never been pulled before." Sam sighed.

Justin laughed. "There's nothing like the initiation into the life of a goalie. You're lucky you got pulled in Bantam. The stakes get higher the further you go. It might be your first, but if you go on in hockey it won't be your last."

Sam nodded. For some reason, he wanted to unload his story. He wanted to get all his feelings off his chest and he couldn't do it with his family or his new friends. He looked up at Justin.

"There's kind of more to it, though," he said.

Justin eyed him.

Sam continued. "My mom broke her leg and didn't come to the game, and neither did my dad because he was out of town. I told them I played great and now my parents are coming to my next game and I'm going to be on the bench. And the coach wants to keep our second goalie in for the next few games."

"So. Talk to your parents."

Sam's mouth opened to retort, but nothing came out. How could the guy just say "SO"? He thought Justin would feel sorry for him. Sam must have looked silly with his mouth open, because Justin burst out laughing.

"Did my brother say some things to you about me?" Sam shoved his hands in his pockets.

Justin shook his head at Sam. "No. But here's a word of advice. The most important thing is how you deal with the crap the next day. If you dwell on it, you'll never be a goalie."

"But I have to sit," said Sam.

"So, I've had to sit before. The first time it happened to me, I whined too. Then my goalie coach, who was an ex-NHLer, pulled me aside and let me have it. He told me to change my attitude and take the opportunity to watch the play." He smiled at Sam. "I bet you learn something."

The Zamboni started up behind them.

"Practice must be over," said Justin. "I gotta go."
"I'd better go too," said Sam.

"You going back to school?"

"No, I think I'll go home and see my folks. I need to talk to them." Sam smiled. "Good luck tonight. Are you starting?"

Justin nodded. "Yup. Hopefully, I play well enough not to get pulled." He playfully punched Sam on the arm. "I'll try to come to another one of your games."

★ ★ ★

Sam arrived home at noon. He pushed open the door and sucked in a huge breath. He didn't want to do this but he had to. His skin felt clammy and his stomach did major flip-flops.

"Sam, is that you?" his mother called from the living room.

"Yeah, it's me," he said. He took off his shoes and hung up his coat.

When he entered the living room, his mother sat on the sofa with her leg propped up on the ottoman. Molly sat curled up in her lap. Had Mom walked all over the house? Seen the mess?

"Sam," she said, frowning. "I told you not to come home today. You're wearing yourself out. I can manage."

"Have you, uh, been in the kitchen yet?"

"Yes," she slowly nodded her head.

"Um, Mom, I've got something to tell you," said Sam. Molly perked up her ears too.

Sam moved to sit beside his mother on the sofa. He reached out to scratch Molly behind the ears. On the walk home, Sam decided to tell about his schoolwork, his hockey, the wrecked laundry, and the jammed closet. He thought maybe he could leave out the part about the dirty dishes in the oven.

"What is it?" She scrunched her eyes and stared at him in obvious concern. "Are you sick?"

"Um," Sam started, "I haven't —"

A noise sounded at the front door.

"Must be your dad," said Mom.

Sam picked at the lint on the blanket that covered his mother. "Dad might as well hear what I have to say too."

"Hey, Sam," said his father. "Mom said you weren't coming home for lunch today."

"I have something to tell you both," said Sam.

★ ★ ★

"Why didn't you tell me you were feeling so stressed?" asked Mom after Sam had explained everything to his parents. He had fessed up to all of it — even the part about skipping school and making a bogus phone call.

He shrugged, feeling the relief of the weight off his shoulders. Why had he carried all that guilt? Why had he thought they wouldn't be on his side? Why had he let it grow and grow, making him do stupid things? "I don't know. I guess I thought I could handle it myself."

Dad put his hand on Sam's shoulder. "Sometimes,

Sam, you have to take help when people offer. It's exactly like playing hockey. You make a great save and one of your teammates has to be in the right position to pick up the rebound. You have to work together."

"I know," said Sam. "So, are you going to ground me? "

Mom smiled. "You've been penalized enough already. We know how hard it is for you to have to sit on the bench. We're still coming to watch, though." She winked.

"You boys could use some cleaning lessons."

"I'm better than Brian," retorted Sam.

"We should make your mom some lunch," Sam's dad said. "Then I'll drive you back to school."

"Okay," said Sam

"How about we make those grilled cheese buns that we put in the oven under the broiler?"

"Um, Dad," said Sam. "I have one more thing to tell you."

15 Sharing Good Advice

Sam sat on the bench. The puck dropped. The Kanata Kings were playing the Nepean Northstars. The Northstars hadn't lost a game yet this season.

The time on the bench had actually been good for Sam, especially since he was new to Ottawa. He wrote notes on all the players: where they liked to shoot from, how they deked, what kind of shots they had. He noted who had the hardest shot, who shot low, who shot high. He got to know who was who by stick and gloves. He also watched each team to see what system they played. When he got home, he'd write everything out so he wouldn't forget. His dad took his own notes and when they got home, they sat down and compared at the kitchen table.

Right off the face-off, the Northstars took posses-sion. They had one player who was so skilled. He was the biggest on the team and also the fastest skater. Sam eyed him, watching him skate down the ice. Then he glanced at Jerry. How was Jerry going to handle him? The guy skated around everyone and was suddenly alone, heading toward Jerry in a breakaway. Jerry crouched. Sam noticed he was bent over a bit too far, something Sam had been corrected on. Jerry looked small in the net.

The player made a lateral move, then deked and fired the puck in the top corner. First shot of the night and it was in the net.

"Jerry, shake it off!" yelled Sam.

Jerry skated out of his net as if trying to get out the early game jitters. Sam always slugged back water, Jerry skated out of his net.

"You can do it," whispered Sam.

This time when the puck dropped, the Kings took possession. Steven sailed down the outside. The defence from the Northstars drilled him along the boards and he crashed to the ice. The puck was loose. Alex swung in, picked it up, did a 180 on his skates, and fired a shot off. It was a super hard shot, but it hit the pads of the Northstars' centre and bounced out. The centre skated forward, pushing the puck with his stick.

The play turned. The guy was on his second breakaway of the night!

Sam held his breath and watched Jerry. From the way he was back in his net, Sam knew he was unsure. Jerry's second shot was going to be another breakaway. What bad luck!

Jerry went down early. The Northstars player roofed the puck and hit the back of the net. When Jerry saw the puck behind the line, he slammed his stick on the ice. Obviously distraught, he skated a circle around his net.

The play resumed at centre ice. Within thirty seconds, Coach Darren called for a line change. As the players raced to the bench, one stepped out before the other stepped in and the puck hit his skate. The whistle blew. Too many men.

Coach Darren jumped off his perch and came down to Sam.

"Get ready," he said. "You could be going in."

Sam picked up his mask and held it tight to his body.

The Northstars took possession off the face-off and immediately took control in the Kings' end zone. The Kings played the box, trying to delay a shot on net. The first Northstars' power-play shot came from the blue line. It was a weak slapshot. When the puck flew into the back of the net, Jerry lowered his head in dejection.

Coach Darren put one foot on the boards and yelled to Jerry, motioning for him to come in. Sam quickly put on his helmet.

When the gate opened, Sam skated out. He held out his glove for Jerry to tap with his own.

In his net, Sam skated back and forth a few times, batted each post, then got in his crouch. He was ready.

Sam's eyes didn't leave the puck. The Northstars took possession and were flying down the ice on a three-on-two. Sam read his ice, read every player. His defence had the wingers covered for now, but they were moving to stay open. Suddenly, the Northstars centre flew over the blue line. The Northstars' winger drop-passed the puck to the centre. The centre wound up for a shot. Sam whipped his glove in the air. When he felt the puck in his glove, he snapped it shut.

First shot, first save.

Steven hit his stick on Sam's pads. "Hey, Hollywood, great save."

Sam nodded.

He ran through his face-off checklist, never taking his eyes off the puck. The Northstars won the face-off and got the puck back.

"Cover in front," yelled Sam. His defence tried to tie up the Northstar forward. The defence took a shot from the point. Partially screened, Sam blocked the shot. It rebounded out. Sticks batted at the puck. Sam kept his eyes glued to it. Finally, he pounced, covered the puck, and ducked his head. He felt the bodies landing on top of him. He cradled the puck into his chest.

The referee screeched to a stop in front of the net and started pulling players off each other. The Kings' defence was adamant about protecting Sam and started shoving. Finally, the ref separated everyone, then fixed

Sam's net. Sam slugged back some water, then snapped down his cage.

This time, the Kings won the face-off and cleared the puck out of their end. Sam watched the play and, when he saw the turn-over, got ready for the next shot on net.

★ ★ ★

The Kings came back to win the game 4–3. When the buzzer sounded to announce the end of the game, the team threw their gloves in the air and dog-piled on Sam.

Underneath all the bodies, Sam laughed.

In the dressing room after the game, Sam noticed Jerry's lowered head. He knew he'd wait to be the last guy out. Sam decided to wait with him.

"Hey," he said to Jerry after everyone had left the dressing room

"I played terrible," said Jerry.

"Don't dwell on one bad game, okay? I did that and it got me nowhere." Sam remembered Justin's advice. "You have to handle the good with the bad."

Jerry leaned back and shook his head in disappointment. "I was playing great, for what? To play lousy again?" He threw his blocker on the ground.

"Jerry, you played some awesome games and you'll

play that way again. I'd never been pulled from a game until I moved to Ottawa."

Jerry eyed him. "Are you serious?"

"It felt awful to be pulled. But I learned a lot by watching. It did me a lot of good." He paused before he continued. "You've made some unbelievable saves."

"Thanks." Jerry held out his hand.

Sam accepted the handshake. "You know what? We'll both be pulled again one day." Sam stood and picked up his equipment. "It's how we deal with it the next day that counts."